<u>Death By Shock</u>

A Josiah Reynolds Mystery
Book Fifteen

Abigail Keam

Worker Bee Press

Special thanks to Melanie Murphy, Liz Hobson, and Judith R. Weckman.

ISBN 978 1 95347803 0
0421

Published in the USA by

Worker Bee Press
P.O. Box 485
Nicholasville, KY 40340

Books By Abigail Keam

Death By A HoneyBee I
Death By Drowning II
Death By Bridle III
Death By Bourbon IV
Death By Lotto V
Death By Chocolate VI
Death By Haunting VII
Death By Derby VIII
Death By Design IX
Death By Malice X
Death By Drama XI
Death By Stalking XII
Death By Deceit XIII
Death By Magic XIV
Death By Shock XV

The Mona Moon Mystery Series
Murder Under A Blue Moon I
Murder Under A Blood Moon II
Murder Under A Bad Moon III
Murder Under A Silver Moon IV
Murder Under A Wolf Moon V
Murder Under A Black Moon VI

Last Chance For Love Romance Series
Last Chance Motel I
Gasping For Air II
The Siren's Call III
Hard Landing IV
The Mermaid's Carol V

1

"Watch what you're doing!" Shaneika snapped.

"Move then," I hissed back.

Shaneika and I were stuck like two peas in a pod falling over each other in a muddy trench.

Since Comanche had retired from horse racing and was now standing at stud, Shaneika had extra time and decided to try her hand at archaeology. As an enthusiastic amateur historian, archaeology was the next logical step for her. She joined the Daniel Boone Archaeological Society and assisted at digs. Shaneika decided her involvement meant that I was involved as well. The Society needed volunteers to dig an area to the west of Fort Boonesborough where freestanding cabins had stood, so Shaneika signed me up.

How could I refuse? As my attorney, Shaneika had saved my tush many times. Now I was pushing *her* tush out of the way. "You broke the string," I complained, glaring at the snapped filament lying limp on the ground. The university's archaeologists had carefully plotted out a grid of squares for us to excavate, and now one entire strand was on the ground.

"I'll put it back. No need to get your panties in a wad." Shaneika climbed out of our little ditch and pulled the string taut again. "There! Good as new, Miss Fussbucket."

I complained, "I don't understand why we are doing this."

"My ancestor, John Todd, came to Kentucky in 1775. His brothers, Levi and Robert Todd, followed."

"I know that, Shaneika. You crow about it often enough."

"I thought you were descended from Levi Todd," Heather said, putting dirt which needed to be sifted through a screen into a bucket.

"And John Todd didn't even come to Boonesborough. He went to Logan's Station," I reminded Shaneika.

"Todd came through here. He just didn't stay here. I bring him up because of his connection to Daniel Boone. Did you know that John Todd was appointed by the one and only 'give me liberty or give me death' Patrick Henry in 1778 as Lt. Commander of Illinois, and that he represented Kentucky in the General Assembly of Virginia in 1778? He introduced bills to emancipate slaves and set aside land for educational purposes."

"That's rich coming from a family of slave owners," I said.

Shaneika pursed her lips in irritation. She was proud of her heritage and connection to her namesake Mary Todd Lincoln and thus to Abraham Lincoln.

Shaneika, her cousin Heather, and I were at Fort Boonesborough trying to locate the fort's original garbage pit which meant their former outhouse location. Since Hunter was still away and I was trying to wean myself off pain medication, I thought it sounded like a fun adventure. Oh, how stupid can one person be?

It had drizzled the night before, and all the trenches the archaeologists had dug were muddy. It was chilly, the porta potty wasn't installed until late in the morning, and the food truck failed to arrive. I was wet, hungry, and aggravated.

Heather Warfield cackled. "You two fight like an old married couple."

I glanced over at Heather, who was thirty-nine and single, financially independent, lived with two rescue cats, and worked in an animal shelter. She was Rubenesque with ivory skin, long brown hair clipped up into a pony tail, large dark expressive eyes that were near-sighted, and a small mouth. Heather's vocabulary spoke of an extensive education, as she had graduated with degrees in political science and economics. So why was Heather working at an animal shelter and not in her fields of expertise? Was it because she was shy and unassuming? I didn't inquire as that would be uncouth, but that wouldn't stop me from asking Shaneika when we were alone. Yep, I'm a nosey cuss.

It was also evident Heather was a huge UK basketball fan from her UK sweatshirt and UK decals on her sunglasses and watch band. She was also a relative of Shaneika's. They were distant cousins.

The Warfields and the Todds were part of the first wave of European pioneers who lived in the Bluegrass and thus accumulated a fortune through land acquisition and hemp crops. Dr. Elisha Warfield dabbled in horse racing and bred the stallion, Lexington, or Big Lex as the locals called him. You see pictures all over the area of Big Lex, who is colored blue. It gives the tourists pause. Why is the horse portrayed as blue? Folklore has it that the ghost of a "blue" Big Lex can be seen grazing in pastures. The apparition acquired its hue from all the bluegrass he has consumed. Kentucky bluegrass has a bluish tint when allowed to grow to full height, which is why the area around Lexington is called the Bluegrass. Quaint story, huh!

Of course, the Warfields and the Todds intermarried with the other pioneer families as did most of the first European families in this area, so Heather and Shaneika have common ancestors. I studied both of them as I carefully trowelled away thin layers of dirt in our pit.

One of the cousins was pale as a Junco's white underbelly, and the other cousin had light copper-colored skin. Heather was shy and introverted while Shaneika was a lioness and, for my money, the best criminal lawyer in the state of Kentucky. Love, hate, devotion, cruelty, racism, classism, slavery, elitism, heartbreak, repression, and struggle had been bound together in a sacred dance throughout Kentucky history, culminating in Shaneika and Heather, polar opposites, but related by blood and history. They were two women who had come to terms with the sins and accomplishments of their ancestors, embracing their shared past.

That's why we were at Fort Boonesborough sifting through mud with a trowel and a paint brush. Shaneika knew her European ancestors' line of descent, but there were gaps with her African heritage. Shaneika wanted to close those gaps and pass the information on to her son, Lincoln.

In Shaneika's office is a letter from Abraham Lincoln to George Rogers Clark Todd (Mary Todd Lincoln's brother), a Confederate officer's sword, daguerreotypes of black women washing at Camp Nelson (a Union military post during the Civil War and now a military cemetery), and other various Civil War artifacts which she claims are family heirlooms. Though Shaneika won't tell me how exactly she is descended from the Todd family, I know I will drag it out of her one day. At the moment, however, moisture from the muck I knelt in was seeping through my jeans causing me to complain, "I'm going back to the van and change. My pants are getting soaked."

"Boo hoo," Shaneika said, sneering as she plucked a pottery shard from the dirt caked on her trowel. "If you change, you'll get those pants filthy as well." She motioned to the field photographer to photograph the find and then she cataloged it.

I grumbled, "This is crazy. We're not finding anything but broken clay pipe stems and animal bone fragments."

"Let's hope they're animals and not my ancestors," Heather teased. She and Shaneika grinned at each other. "You know the settlers at Jamestown, Virginia resorted to cannibalism."

"Lovely," I replied.

Shaneika said, "Did you know my ancestor John Todd commanded a group of 182 frontiersmen against the British and Shawnee in retaliation for an attack on Bryan Station?"

"Here we go again about John Todd," I murmured.

"What was that?" Shaneika asked.

I said in a louder voice, "We all know about the Battle of Blue Licks in 1782, which is considered the last battle of the Revolutionary War even though the war was officially over." I put another clay pipe stem into a bag and marked it on my grid paper. The information marked on the paper would later be put into a computer.

"I bring it up because Daniel Boone accompanied

John Todd and wanted to wait for reinforcements before engaging the enemy."

Heather looked at Shaneika. "I'm not familiar with this story. Just bits and pieces. What happened then?"

"Some hothead named Hugh McGary accused the men of being cowards and got them riled up, so they attacked. Daniel Boone was remembered to have said, 'We are all slaughtered men now.'"

I said, "A bunch of testosterone driven men who got themselves and their kinfolk dead in my opinion. Of course, Hugh McGary survived. He just had everyone else killed."

Shaneika ignored me and continued regaling us with the Battle of Blue Licks. "Boone was right. It was a trap and they should have waited for reinforcements which were a day away. Not only was John Todd killed, but several members of the Boone family as well, including Daniel Boone's son, Israel. Daniel Boone caught a riderless horse and tried to give it to his son. The story goes that Israel was hesitant to leave his father and in those few seconds was shot to death. Boone then jumped on the horse and rode to safety. Boone had to come back days later to reclaim his son's body and take him to Boone's Station to be buried. There's a stone memorial to Israel Boone still standing. In a battle that lasted less than ten minutes, seventy-two frontiersmen were dead and eleven captured by the Shawnee and the British force."

"Israel's not buried here at Fort Boonesborough?" Heather asked, looking up from her digging.

"I thought Israel was buried at the battle site," I said.

Shaneika said, "No, he's buried at Boone's Station. There's nothing there anymore, but a stone memorial and a historical marker. John Todd is buried in a common grave at the battle site. There is a memorial to all the men who died."

"I find Daniel Boone a controversial figure," Heather said. "Wasn't he adopted by the Shawnee at one point and rumored to have had a Shawnee wife?"

"Some historians believe that he was adopted by the great Shawnee chief, Blackfish, himself. As for a Shawnee wife, who knows? Probably."

I looked at Heather. "I thought you knew all this."

Heather replied, "I know very little about the frontiersmen's period, except for my family. I like to concentrate on history from 1860 through the Reconstruction period."

"Oh," I said. "Well then you might not know that Daniel Boone was not the only one playing around. There is speculation that Edward Boone, Daniel's brother, got Rebecca Boone pregnant while Daniel was on a two year long hunt. Of course, I don't blame Rebecca. She thought Daniel was dead. It's just that Edward Boone was married to her sister Martha, and they were both pregnant around the same time."

"Yikes," Heather said, laughing. "Messy. I wonder what those family get-togethers were like. What did Daniel Boone say when he got back and found a wee babe in the crib?"

"Not much. It seemed Daniel Boone accepted some of the responsibility since he was away for so long and recognized the child as his own. In fact, Jemima was considered his favorite child."

Heather asked, "Is this the scandal that caused Boone to have a falling out with Boonesborough?"

"No, that was due to the aftermath of the Great Siege of Boonesborough. That story had to do with the need for salt from Blue Licks. Boone was considered a Tory and was later court-martialed for treason, but he was acquitted. The trial left Boone so bitter, he moved to his son's small community named Boone's Station near Athens. The Battle of Blue Licks happened four years later than the Great Siege."

"Sounds like Blue Licks was not a lucky place for the Boones," Heather commented.

"I believe I was speaking about my illustrious ancestor, John Todd when I was so rudely interrupted," Shaneika complained, bumping me with her elbow.

"Sorry," I said, looking sheepish. "I do have a tendency to go on."

Looking smug at my apology, Shaneika continued, "As I was saying, seventy-two frontiersmen were killed at the Battle of Blue Licks including John Todd. He was thirty-two years old."

"My gosh, that is young," I said. "And he was a colonel?"

Shaneika said, "Life expectancy was short, so they got on with the business of living. Daniel Boone's daughter, Susannah, was fourteen when she married. Many think she had the first white baby in Kentucky."

"You said 'white baby.' I guess that means something," I alleged.

"The first non-indigenous baby to be born in Kentucky is thought to have been Frederick, a baby born to Dolly, a slave, and her master Richard Callaway in 1775."

"That doesn't sound like a pleasant story," Heather said, looking at Shaneika in dismay. "Do you think they loved each other?"

Shaneika snorted, "For God's sake, get real, Heather. You know what that relationship was about."

I didn't comment because sex between slave owners and slaves was a touchy subject. I didn't like the thought of those poor women's plight or any woman in sexual jeopardy. As a female, it made me uncomfortable. Made me want to take a gun and shoot some man.

The three of us returned to our work, reflecting quietly on the hardships women endured in pioneer life—hardships women have always endured.

"A pipe bowl this time. Did these men do nothing but smoke? And where did they get the tobacco? I haven't read any accounts of tobacco being grown at Fort Boonesborough," I sputtered, sticking the bowl stem in another bag.

Shaneika said, "The women smoked as well. I think when they ran out of tobacco, they smoked other plants. Besides sex and eating, what pleasures did these people have? There was no TV. No restaurants. No spas. No sports. No movies. No theater. No concerts. Not even the simple pleasures of bathing. The women and children couldn't even go outside the fort for a walk. I read somewhere that a woman recounted for a historian that as a child, her mother wouldn't let her leave the fort for over two years because it was too dangerous. Two years!"

"If you put it that way, I guess smoking was one of the few enjoyments they had to counteract the endless work and stress," I said, reaching back and feeling the back of my pants. "Oh, the moisture is soaking through to my panties now. Ugh."

"You sure it's not you losing control?" Shaneika teased.

"I'm not there yet, but give me a few years. As one gets older, all the orifices loosen. Just you wait. Your turn will come."

Heather asked, "If you don't like to excavate, Josiah, why did you come?"

"Josiah is detoxing from pain medication while Hunter is away," Shaneika shot back.

"Is Hunter your gentleman friend, Josiah?" Heather asked, grinning at me. "How serious is your relationship? Come on. Spill it."

"Gee, thanks, Shaneika. I don't think the people over in the next county heard you imply that I am a drug addict," I hissed back, resisting the urge to thump Shaneika on her newly shaved head or pull out one of her large hoop earrings, this being her current look. She was the only woman I knew who changed hairstyles like some women change purses.

"Are you really addicted to drugs?" Heather asked, her large eyes widening.

Wiggling her eyebrows, Shaneika added, "Pain medication."

I replied, "Let's say I'm trying to improve my health and leave it at that." Taking a breather, I looked around. "Boy, I'd really like a drink right now."

"True junkie talk. One drug substituting for another."

"You know, Shaneika, I'm gonna punch your self-righteous snout right in your nose."

Shaneika turned and stared at me. "That makes no sense, Josiah. A snout *is* a nose."

"You know what I mean."

"You better not be having a stroke, because I'm not gonna drag your white fanny out of this pit."

"Yeah?"

"Yeah."

"Make me."

"Girls! Ladies! Behave!" Heather insisted. "Decorum at all times when in public."

Shaneika and I both turned to Heather and yelled, "SHUT UP!"

Heather's face turned crimson.

Ashamed that we had hurt Heather's feelings, I said, "Don't worry, Heather. No one is looking at us. Everyone is staring at the twins." I was referring to the two fabulous women occupying the pit on the other side of the site. They were the Dane twins, both identical with pale skin, startlingly light blue eyes, athletic figures, and ebony hair with a shock of gray at their widow peaks. I couldn't tell if the gray shock was natural or artificial. As I stated before, they were identical. I could never tell them apart.

"What's their story again?" Shaneika asked.

I replied, "I know them well enough to say hello and that's it. I met them once through Lady Elsmere at one of her parties. I doubt they would remember me."

Heather eagerly glanced about to see if anyone was listening to our conversation. Seeing that everyone seemed intent upon their work, she spoke in a stage whisper, "The Dane twins are from Baltimore, and their father was an industrialist who worked for the Navy. Apparently, he supplied them with some type of screw they needed and made a fortune. Of course, that was years back. These girls are from his second marriage late in life."

"They are hardly girls," Shaneika commented, looking at them from the corner of her eye. "More like late thirties or early forties."

"They are thirty-five," Heather said.

I said, "Hmm. They look older."

"They partied very hard when young, and tragedy has followed them throughout their lives," Heather explained. "Haven't you heard of the Dane curse?"

"It's a novel by Dashiell Hammett."

"No, Josiah, this is for real," Heather insisted.

"Like how?" I asked, suddenly interested. Talk of curses always fascinated me.

"Both wives of Mr. Dane died from accidents. The first Mrs. Dane died in a skiing accident. She collided with a tree."

"Holy moly, that's harsh," Shaneika said.

"The second Mrs. Dane died in a car accident when her chauffeur drove off a cliff. There were rumors the two were involved, and the 'accident' was really a murder/suicide when she refused to leave old man Dane."

"Wow," I said.

"Double wow," Shaneika said, putting down her trowel and staring at the Dane women.

I slapped her foot. "You're ogling."

Shaneika countered, "I'm not ogling. I'm studying them."

"You're gawking."

"They might need a sharp lawyer for their legal

team. I'm going over there and hand them my card."
Shaneika stared at my astonished face. "Well, you never
know. Josiah, since you know them, you must intro-
duce me to them."

"Like I told you, I've met them once for a brief
introduction. I hardly call that knowing them. Not only
can I not tell them apart, I don't remember their
names."

"It's Magda and Maja," Heather offered, "but the
story doesn't end with the second Mrs. Dane's death."

"There's more?" I asked.

"Quite a bit, I'm afraid," Heather said. "Before old
man Dane died, he discovered one of his adult children
from his first marriage was embezzling from the family
firm, and he disinherited him. Ultimately the embezzler
died from a drug overdose. Apparent suicide."

"How many children did Mr. Dane have in all?"
Shaneika asked.

Looking smug, Heather replied, "Five. One died in
infancy."

"Another whammy," Shaneika commented.

"How do you know all of this, Heather?" I asked,
bagging more animal bones before marking their
location on a grid survey. I motioned for a volunteer to
carry the bones away for analysis.

"I read the *New York Times* and the *Wall Street Jour-
nal*. The Dane family has been written about ad
nauseam."

"I never heard of the family before meeting the twins," I said. "I don't know how I could have missed all this drama. It's right up my alley."

"I'm not finished," Heather said.

Shaneika exclaimed. "There's more?"

"Yeah, a real cliffhanger."

"Ugh, Heather, enough with the references to cliffs, please," I complained.

"Sorry, Josiah. I forget you fell off a cliff yourself."

I remarked, "My stomach is turning."

"You gotta hear this though. It turned out that old man Dane disinherited all of his children, except for Magda, the older of the twins."

Shaneika asked, "He did this why?"

"Magda has a real knack for business, and he felt she would preserve the family business and fortune. He was right. The Dane brand has expanded under her leadership—tech companies, facial recognition software, robotic firms—stuff to do with national security."

"Even though Magda expanded the company, it would still piss me off if I were Maja," Shaneika offered.

I asked, "What about the other Dane offspring?"

"The older sister from the first marriage keeps out of the limelight. She has a cottage on Martha's Vineyard."

"What's her name?" I asked.

"Margot, I think," Heather replied, staring at the twins.

Shaneika said, "Magda controls her siblings because she holds the family purse strings. That's what I would do to make them behave and keep them at arms length."

"And Maja?" I asked, amused that Heather seemed to be a crime buff.

"She lives in the guest house on the family estate in Baltimore, where the family firm is still located. I think they live on an island in the bay."

Shaneika asked, "Why not inside the family home?"

"Magda lives there with her husband, Gavin McCloud."

I clucked, "Imagine having your own island in Chesapeake Bay."

Shaneika turned to me. "Sounds similar to the Lee case you were involved in a few months back. By the way, is Hunter still working on that case?"

"He called the other night and said that Rudy Lee's partner in crime, Lettie Lemore pleaded guilty to illegal drug distribution and evidence tampering in a plea deal. The DA dropped the charge for conspiracy to commit murder in the death of Johnny Stompanato, but she still refused to talk about Lee. We might never know how Lee really died."

"What are you two talking about?" Heather asked.

"An acquaintance of Josiah's who died a month or

so ago. That's all."

Heather looked confused. "You must tell me, Jo. I didn't read about it in the paper."

"There was a little article about the man's death in the paper. The reporter has since quit Lexington and relocated to Las Vegas."

"Was it murder?"

"Don't know. Death was ruled inconclusive."

Heather said, "I don't know how you do it, Josiah. You keep your cool so. I would just fall apart seeing a dead body. I really would. And the confrontations you have had with murderers. I would freeze. I know I would. You know I keep up with you in the papers. You've got a reputation for solving murders. I confess I'm quite a fan." She leaned over in a conspiratorial fashion. "What are the details of your friend's death? Leave nothing out."

"He wasn't my friend, but I'll tell you about it another time, Heather. I see the food truck has arrived. I'm going to get something."

I needed to eat. I was getting the shakes from weaning myself off so much pain medication. Food helped with the withdrawal—mainly booze and chocolate, the important food groups.

Just breathe, Josiah, I told myself. *Just breathe. You'll be all right.*

2

I grudgingly got up off my knees. In fact, Shaneika had to pull me up. As soon as I was steady on my feet, I said, "Well, come on, girls. I'm buying. My treat."

Shaneika threw down her trowel and stepped out of the trench. "Sounds good to me. I could do with a cup of coffee." She extended her hand to Heather. "Come on, Cousin Heather. Let's take a break."

Heather and Shaneika followed me to the truck where we got in line behind four other volunteers. As soon as it was my turn to order, one of the Dane twins stepped in front of me and proceeded to place her order. Flabbergasted, I turned to face Shaneika and Heather with my mouth open.

Shaneika was the first to speak up. "Excuse me, but this lady was in front of you." When the twin ignored her, Shaneika spoke up more forcefully, "Hey, white girl. I'm talkin' to you. You need to get to the back of the line."

The Dane twin twisted around slowly and

ABIGAIL KEAM

disdainfully looked the three of us up and down. "Would you be addressing me?"

"You cut in front of us. There is a line," I said, keeping my voice low and evenly modulated as I didn't want to cause a scene. I pointed to the line behind me.

"So I did," the woman replied, as she turned away from me and paid the food truck server. Giving me a smirk, the Dane twin took a bite of her barbeque sandwich before walking away.

"Well, of all the nerve," Heather sputtered. The three of us watched the twin sashay toward a picnic table.

"May I help you?" the irritated server asked, totally unaware of what had taken place. His only concern was to keep the line moving.

"Sorry," I replied. "I would like three barbeque sandwiches, three fries, two waters, and one large coffee, please." As I paid for the food, Shaneika helped carry it over to a table far away from the Dane woman. Heather followed with the condiments. The three of us huddled together, but I couldn't enjoy my sandwich. I was too angry.

I must have been wearing my emotions on my sleeve because Heather said, "Anger is bad for the digestive system. Let it go."

"I hate bullies," I replied.

"So do I," Shaneika said, seething.

Heather smiled sweetly, "Cuz, you are an officer of

20

the court. You can't do anything about this. Both of you, let it go. The Dane woman's not worth any trouble."

"Do you know which one she is, Heather?"

"No, I have trouble telling them apart."

"I think it was Maja. She parts her hair on the left," I replied.

Shaneika spoke up, "You couldn't remember their names, but you remember which twin parted her hair in a particular way?"

"Once Heather reminded me of their names, I remembered."

Heather offered, "They might not be consistent with how they style their hair. They may switch it up to fool people."

I said, "True. Didn't think of that."

Changing the subject, Shaneika suggested, "Why don't we go kayaking on the river tomorrow evening? I hear the other volunteers are getting a group together. Kentucky is so pretty in the spring. The redbuds and dogwoods are blooming now."

"No thanks, Shaneika," Heather said. "You know I'm not a fan of water. Besides, it's still too cold. I had to wear a coat this morning."

"You'll have a life jacket on, Heather. Even if you fall in, you'll bob back up. You can kayak with me. I'll keep you safe."

"Again, no thanks, Shaneika. Water sports are not

my thing. I get nervous just looking at water."

"You big baby." Shaneika looked at me.

"I'm out, too. Getting in and out of a kayak has me flummoxed. It's all I can do to get up on a horse, and that is with steps and stable hands to help me."

"Too bad, but I think I'll join the others tomorrow." Shaneika looked up at the darkening sky. "That is if I get up early enough. I feel tired today. I may sleep in."

"Hello ladies. Taking a break, I see."

The three of us looked up to see Dr. Reese smiling at us. She was the archaeologist in charge of the dig. Unlike me, she had dressed appropriately for the dig. Dr. Reese was wearing some sort of plastic overalls over her clothes, boots, a neck scarf, and gloves. Her chestnut hair was piled up into a bun, although loose strands danced about her tanned oval face. I approximated Dr. Reese to be about forty.

"Hello, Dr. Reese. Would you like to join us?" I asked, when to my surprise Heather kicked me under the table.

"No, thank you. Just came to get some coffee. Everybody doing okay?"

"Sure," I said.

Shaneika asked, "Has anyone found any artifacts specific to African Americans?"

Dr. Reese shook her head. "Nothing with any names on it. Sorry, Shaneika. I know that is your focus."

"Were there many slaves at Boonesborough?" I asked, rubbing my sore shin and giving Heather a dirty look.

"More than you would think. Boonesborough even had free black men taking their chances as early as 1775. In fact, a free black man by the name of Richard Hines built a cabin not too far from here. Unfortunately, he built it near a known river crossing for the Shawnee and was killed in 1779. The river bend on his property is still referred to as Hines Bend. Another free man, who came early, was John Sidebottom. He fought in the Revolutionary War and is credited with saving future president, James Monroe, at the Battle of Trenton."

I said, "I'm not too keen on my colonial history. Isn't that the battle when George Washington crossed the Delaware River on Christmas night and captured a contingent of Hessians?"

Dr. Reese said, "Yes. Have you seen the painting of it by Emanuel Leutze? I can never look at that painting without getting chills."

Dr. Reese laid her hand on Shaneika's shoulder. "I'm afraid there is very little written about the women in this period, especially black women. One reason is that most people couldn't read or write. Even those who could didn't write in their diaries about their wives or daughters unless they married, had children, or died. The few good bio details we have of most pioneer women were written down if they had been stolen by Native Americans—a prime example being Jenny Wiley. Rebecca Boone is the only pioneer woman in Kentucky that we have solid biographical information on. For other women, we must glean information from wills, petitions, family bibles, and stories handed down in families. We're not sure about how many black women were at Fort Boonesborough. We know only a few of their names, but we know there were black women here in the beginning."

"Is there a list of Monk Estill's children?" Shaneika asked. "I'm wondering if there is a connection between his descendants and the Todd family."

"You can find what information we have on him in the Kentucky Historical Society in Frankfort. He did have three wives and thirty children."

"I've heard that name before, but don't know much about him," I said.

Dr. Reese seemed happy to oblige. "Monk was James Estill's slave and extremely vital to the survival of Boonesborough. You might call him a Renaissance man. Not that he was a formal scholar, but a man of many talents. He made rugs and blankets out of elk and bison hides, planted apple orchards, and most important of all, mined saltpeter and guano for gunpowder. Without gunpowder, the settlers would not have survived. He was also known for his strength and bravery. He once carried a wounded man twenty-five miles to safety. When James Estill was killed by the Shawnee in 1782, his son Wallace, freed Monk and provided for him until his death in 1835."

I asked, "What did Monk do after he was set free?"

"He became a Baptist minister," Dr. Reese replied.

Unexpectantly, Heather said tersely, "It looks like it's going to rain, Dr. Reese."

I shot Heather another look and noticed Shaneika seemed tense.

Dr. Reese looked at the sky. "It does look threatening, doesn't it, Heather? One should be careful of storms lest one is carried away by the tempest."

I thought that an odd thing to say, but then I think people are strange.

Heather looked away while Shaneika looked uncomfortable.

"Well, I'd better get back." Dr. Reese waved goodbye and hurried back to the site.

"What was that about, Heather? Why did you kick me?" I asked.

"Did I? I'm so sorry. It was an accident."

"It hurt."

"I'm sorry, Josiah. Very sorry."

"You got something against Dr. Reese?"

Shaneika intervened, saying, "Look, the rain is coming."

"Naw, it will hold off until this evening," I said, right before a big raindrop splashed into my eye.

"That does it," Shaneika said, grabbing her food. "Let's retire to my RV."

I dumped my Styrofoam container into a garbage bin and hurried to Shaneika's rented RV. I spied the archaeologists pulling large tarps over the dig as I rushed to get out of the drizzle. It seemed they were done for the day.

So was I.

3

Since I needed to work the farmer's market in Lexington the next morning, I met up with Shaneika on Thursday at Fort Boonesborough. The fort is really not that far from my house, the Butterfly, if one drives across the ferry at Valley View. I parked my newly refurbished VW van next to Shaneika's sleek RV and popped up a few chairs around a campfire. We took advantage of the campgrounds adjacent to the fort, to save us driving time the four days we were committed to the project. That was all the money and time the archaeologists' grant allowed. Four days. The only time I couldn't help with the dig was when I had to go into town for the market on Saturday.

The rain had stopped, so Heather, Shaneika, and I perched in front of a fire roasting marshmallows when a stunning looking woman approached us. *Oh, what fresh hell is this?* I thought as I recognized her as one of the Dane twins.

"Hello," she said in a melodious voice. She obviously had elocution lessons in the past. "May I join you for a moment?"

"Sure," Heather invited. "Pull up a chair."

I inwardly groaned.

"Thank you." She sat and looked at us expectantly.

We stared back at her. Silence fell over our group as we were waiting for each other to speak.

"My name is Josiah," I said, finally. "These crazy gals are Heather and Shaneika."

"I know you, Josiah," the Dane woman said. "Well, I don't know you, but we've met before at one of Lady Elsmere's to-dos."

"I'm surprised you remembered. That was a long time ago."

"It seems like a lifetime," the Dane woman mused. "I keep up with you in the papers. You're quite famous as a sleuth. It must be fascinating to solve all those murder cases."

"You get the local paper?"

"I subscribe to papers from all over the country. A woman in my position needs to know what is going on in the world and who the players are."

I was amazed that I was considered a player. "I'm sorry, but I don't remember which twin you are."

The Dane woman laughed. It was an easy laugh without pretense.

It made me relax a little and feel kindly toward her.

"That's why I'm here. I saw my sister jump in front

of you at the food truck, and I would like to apologize on behalf of my family. My sister can be a little—" she paused for a moment searching for the right word— "impetuous."

"Are you going to tell me that she didn't see the line?"

"Heavens no. I won't make excuses, but I would like to apologize."

I said, "It was a lousy thing to do, especially when it's hard for me to stand for any period of time."

The woman sighed. She was used to getting her way and didn't like to be challenged.

Star-struck, Heather stuck out her hand. "Let's start over. I'm Heather. This is my cousin, Shaneika, and you know Josiah."

The Dane woman smiled and shook hands with Heather. "Hi, I'm Magda Dane McCloud."

I gathered a cup and poured bourbon in it, offering it to the Dane twin. "Here, Magda. This will put hair on your chest."

"Thank you," Magda said, taking the paper cup gratefully. She gingerly sniffed the bourbon before imbibing.

As Magda took a sip, Baby, my big lumbering dog, woke from his nap and stumbled out of my van, looking for fun and food. Of course, Baby was with me. You didn't think I'd leave him at home, did you?

Magda almost spilled her drink when she saw Baby.

She was startled as are most people when they first lay eyes on him. You would never believe how many people mistake Baby for a lioness.

"He's gentle," I reassured.

"He's an English Mastiff?"

"Yes. His name is Baby."

"Some baby," Magda said. "How many pounds?"

"About two hundred twenty. Somewhere in that area."

Magda laughed, "You must be feeding him well. He's huge."

"Yep, Baby is a big boy."

Hearing me say his name, Baby leaned into me and whimpered. I gave him a cooled-off roasted marshmallow. "That's all."

He whimpered some more.

"No," I said. "Marshmallows are not good for you."

Magda asked, "May I pet him?"

"Just call his name. He'll come right to you. I should caution you that Baby drools quite a bit."

Magda called to him.

Baby turned and saw Magda motioning to him. Thinking she might offer him a treat, Baby padded over and rested his massive head upon her lap.

"He likes to be scratched behind the ears," I said.

Magda cautiously petted Baby. "His fur is so soft," she said, looking up at me. "Oh, he is a lovely boy. I love dogs. Animals of all sorts. I wish I had time for them."

"You shouldn't have told me that. I'm going to tell Lady Elsmere, and she'll hit you up for a large donation to her new animal sanctuary," I said. "Are you staying in the campground or in town?"

"My husband and I are four doors down in the silver and red RV. My sister, Maja, and the rest of the family are staying in a B&B nearby."

Shaneika and I swiveled to stare at the gleaming RV that took up two spots due to its huge size. I wondered how it could be driven. It was as large as a semi truck.

"Magda, I thought you had retired," Heather said, "or, at least, slacked off a little bit."

"What made you think that?" Magda asked, still petting Baby. She avoided eye contact with Heather.

"I haven't seen much written about you lately in the papers and because you are here. Isn't your company located in Baltimore?"

Shaneika added, "Yes, why are you here in Kentucky and at Fort Boonesborough on a dig?"

"You guys caught me. Dr. Reese and I are in the same college sorority. She sent out a bulletin asking for volunteers, so I thought to myself—why not? And you are correct about me wishing to retire. I want to live in this area, so I'm using this excavation as an excuse to have a look-see."

"Because of the horse farms?" I asked.

"It's so pretty here," Magda said, "and, yes, because of the horse farms. I've been looking at a few for sale. I don't want to race horses or breed them. I want to open up a nursery for pregnant brood mares."

"There are several farms which offer that service already," Shaneika said.

"But mostly for Thoroughbreds. I want to offer the service to Standardbreds and other breeds as well."

"Horse owners don't like to put different breeds of horses in the same pastures," Heather said. "Thoroughbreds are notoriously temperamental."

"I'm aware of that. I'll make sure they are separated."

Shaneika hammered away, "But why volunteer for this little dig besides being a friend of Dr. Reese? You must have your choice of archaeological digs worldwide."

"I'm a student of American history and am fascinated with Kentucky. Its history is so cursed and bloody. I am ashamed to say the macabre captivates me. I also wanted to get my sisters and my husband into an area where we could have privacy. I'm about to announce something rather important, and I wanted them away from the limelight with time to absorb my news and think."

"Then you are selling the family business," Heather surmised.

Magda's eyes widened. "How did you guess?"

"It's the only thing that makes sense."

"Please don't tell anyone. I beg you. The announcement will be made in two weeks, although the deal will go into effect on Monday after I sign some papers. I wanted my family away from influences that might make this transition more difficult for them."

"Is the rest of your family here?" Heather asked.

"My other sister is flying in tonight. Neither sister has any idea about the sale, and I want to keep it that way until I tell them this weekend."

"If I were you, I would tell your husband immediately. You're going to need someone to have your back, especially when money and family are involved," I cautioned.

"Is your lawyer going to be present?" Shaneika asked.

Magda shook her head. "I just wanted family present this weekend."

"Present for what?" a deep voice boomed from behind us.

We looked up to see a tall man standing a few feet beyond us with a darkening sky behind him. He was handsome, although his beauty was fading. The skin on his patrician features looked slacked and yellowish. He was wearing clean khakis with a white shirt which showed off his dyed dark hair and luminous black eyes. I could tell that in his youth, the man had been arm candy. Even I would have turned to watch him pass me on the street.

"Magda was just telling us the family is getting together for a reunion," I said.

Magda shot me a grateful look.

Ignoring the rest of us, the man spoke to Magda sharply, "Darling, we must be going if we are to meet them at the hotel for dinner. I got word that Margot has arrived."

Magda turned away from her husband, explaining, "Margot is my older sister. She flew in from New England."

"Magda!" Gavin said, tapping the face of his Rolex wristwatch.

Embarrassed at Gavin's rudeness, Magda rose. "Everyone, please meet my husband, Gavin McCloud. Gavin, going left to right is Shaneika, Heather, and Josiah."

Gavin nodded hello to us while giving me a hard look. "Have we met before?"

I nodded. "Lady Elsmere's party several years ago. You came in for the Kentucky Derby."

"And your name again?"

"Josiah Reynolds."

Gavin made the connection. "The woman with a man's name." Making the connection, he snapped his fingers. "You're the lady detective."

Before I could respond, he swung over to Shaneika, "And you had a horse running in the Derby. Lost by a nose. Gawd, what a race that was. You must have been pissed." Gavin gave a hearty chuckle. "There was something else. Oh, I remember now. You got into an argument at Lady Elsmere's Derby ball with some other horseman by the name of, hmm, let me think. Let me think. It will come to me," he said, snapping his fingers again.

"Charlie Hoskins," Heather piped up.

He pointed at Shaneika. "Yeah, that's right. Charlie Hoskins. His horse was the favorite. Didn't he get arrested in the Caribbean for some shady dealing with that horse?"

Shaneika shot Gavin a withering look.

Seeing the ire in Shaneika's eyes, Magda changed the subject. "And this furry monster is Josiah's dog. I'm sorry. What's his name again?"

Before I could answer, Gavin said, "Well, nice to meet you all." He gave us all a perfect smile with expensive, capped teeth before imploring Magda, "Baby, we've gotta go. We're late as it is."

Hearing his name, Baby went over to Gavin expecting a treat or a pet; whereupon, Gavin pushed him away. "Can someone control this animal?"

"Come here, Baby," I said, holding a peanut butter treat in my hand. Baby gave Gavin a hurt look before trotting over to me.

Magda gave a weak smile. "Thanks again for the drink, ladies. Please give Lady Elsmere our regards. I hope she is doing well."

"She is," I replied. "She'll be sorry that she missed

your visit to Kentucky."

Watching Gavin stride off, Magda said, "See you all tomorrow."

"Good evening," we said to the now retreating couple as Magda walked briskly to catch up with Gavin.

As soon as they were out of earshot, Shaneika said, "Now that was truly odd."

"Why?" Heather asked, putting another marshmallow on her stick.

"The entire conversation was bizarre."

"I don't understand," Heather said, poking her marshmallow into the fire.

"First of all, how do we know that is really Magda? Those two twins dress and look alike," Shaneika argued.

Heather said, "She identified Gavin as her husband, and he identified the woman as his wife. Of the siblings, only Magda has the old ball and chain tied to her ankle. The rest never married or are divorced."

"But Gavin didn't identify the woman as his wife. Just called her darling and baby," I said.

"But he did," Heather insisted.

I said, "You're right. He called her Magda."

"My goodness, you two are so suspicious of everyone," Heather said. "Josiah, do you really think that wasn't Magda Dane?"

"I'm sure it was Magda Dane," I said, laughing. "She wasn't the woman who jumped in front of me at the food truck. Our visitor's demeanor was completely different. Besides, she liked Baby and Baby took to her. Good enough character reference for me."

Heather looked confused.

I said, "We're just putting you on, Heather."

"It still doesn't prove that the woman who apologized was Magda Dane. It only proves the twins have dissimilar personalities," Shaneika argued. "And you can't prove it by DNA since they are identical."

"Will you stop being a lawyer, cuz?" Heather said, pulling a gooey charred marshmallow off her stick and popping it into her mouth.

"I think what makes Shaneika so suspicious is Magda telling us that she had sold the family business," I said, putting a hotdog on my stick after giving a raw one to Baby. "That is very big news. Why would she tell three complete strangers something so important? We could call the newspapers and let the cat out of the bag before Monday, which could screw the deal or make the stock market slide. Telling us that scoop is not something an astute business person would do."

"I concur," Shaneika said. "Magda came over with the intent to tell us about her selling out and not to apologize for her sister."

Heather grabbed the Graham crackers and chocolate, making herself a S'more. "Maybe she's lonely."

I wanted to roll my eyes at Heather's naivety, but resisted. Instead, I patted Heather's knee. "You're probably right, honey." I yawned. "Guys, I've had too much bourbon and it's making me sleepy, so I'm turning in. I'll be back after the market is over tomorrow and finish out Saturday and Sunday on the dig."

"Good night," Heather said. "Pleasant dreams."

"See ya tomorrow," Shaneika said.

I locked up my van and wandered over to Shaneika's RV where I was staying for the weekend. Baby followed obediently and immediately jumped into our small bunk bed while I took a quick shower before retiring.

I did have pleasant dreams that night.

It was the next day that turned into a nightmare.

4

I got up around six and took Baby for a tinkle walk into the woods away from the campgrounds. The sun was coming up. I looked at my watch. It was getting late, and it would take me an hour to get to the market. If I was tardy for the setup time, the market wouldn't let me sell. I needed to hurry.

As Baby and I were heading back, Heather rushed out of the woods and ran toward me, waving frantically. She looked flushed and frightened. Catching up with me and gasping for air, Heather grabbed my arm and pulled. "Come, Josiah. We must get away."

When someone says to run, I run. Danger is everywhere.

Heather raced ahead and burst into Shaneika's RV. I followed, looking behind, but saw nothing before dashing into the RV. Now catching my breath, I slumped into a chair and asked, "What was it, Heather? A bear?"

"Something evil."

"Evil? A bear is not evil. A bear is just a bear."

Heather swallowed. "I went into the woods to do some bird watching."

I noticed the binoculars around Heather's neck. "I see."

"Around dawn, birds are very active. That's when I like to watch for them."

"Okay."

Heather leaned toward me and whispered, "I saw Gavin kissing Maja in the woods, and overhead them plotting to kill Magda."

I drew back. "What!"

"I caught Gavin and Maja plotting to kill Magda."

"Did they see you?"

"I don't think so."

"Tell me everything you saw and heard."

"I was looking for Pileated Woodpeckers when I spied Gavin kissing a woman through my binoculars."

"Then what?"

"I crept closer."

"Heather, it's not proper to spy on two people making love."

"You are lecturing me about protocol after all the naughty things you have done."

"Point taken."

"As I was saying, I crept closer and heard Maja say, 'Let's do this. We can make it look like an accident. No one will suspect.'"

"And did the man say anything?"

"He said something like, 'Okay, but we have to do it soon. Before Monday. I told you she was going ahead with this. If she does, all is lost. I'll have nothing.'"

"Are you sure that's what they said?"

"I admit they were far away, but you know how sound travels along the Palisades. I'm sure that's what they said. You can whisper and a person can hear plainly what you've said a hundred yards away."

"Okay, Heather. I believe you. You saw something that has upset you, but you need to be positive. This is a serious charge. Are you positive the people who you saw were Gavin and Maja?"

Heather hesitated for a second. "I think so. The light was dim filtering through the trees, and they were in the shadows. But if it wasn't Maja, why would Gavin and Magda be kissing in the woods at six in the morning when they have a huge motor home parked in the campgrounds?" Heather grabbed my hand. "What should I do? It was alarming to hear such things."

I nibbled on the side of my lip and resisted looking at my watch. I could tell Heather was very upset. "Listen, Heather. I need to leave, or I'm going to be late for work. Shaneika will be up soon. Tell her everything you've told me, and let Shaneika handle this. Until you tell her, keep this RV locked and don't go outside. I'm trusting Gavin and Maja didn't see you, but let's play it safe, just in case."

"You don't believe me. I can tell."

"I believe you saw and heard something, and I've had enough experience with human nature to know people will do anything if they feel threatened, especially about money. I'll be back around two. Just stay inside the RV until I get back."

"I'm telling the truth, Josiah."

"I know you are, honey, and it will be dealt with, but I've got to go. I'll be back soon." I kissed her on her forehead. "Don't worry, Heather. Shaneika and I will take care of this. We'll sort this out."

And so I left.

How stupid could I have been?

The nightmare had begun to unfold, but I didn't realize it.

5

I had a good day selling honey and sold out my fifteen cartons of boutique eggs. My hens were laying well, so I planned to buy more chickens. People loved my concept of multi-colored eggs in a reusable and biodegradable carton making the eggs a big hit. I had to establish myself as the premier boutique egg lady quickly before other farmers copied my idea. My head was brimming with ideas as I drove down I-75 toward Richmond in my newly renovated VW van with Baby sitting in the back seat. Humming to the radio, I got off the expressway and turned on the road to Fort Boonesborough. I sang in baby talk, "Hey Baby, I've got a purse full of wonderful sweaty cash, and I'm going to spend some of it on you. Yes, I am. Yes, I am." As I turned into the campground road, the main entrance was blocked by a police car. Stopping my van, I rolled down the window and poked my head out as a Madison County policeman came toward me.

"Sorry, ma'am, but the campgrounds are closed

until further notice."

"I have a spot here. I only left this morning to attend to business. What has happened?" My heart was pumping fast and sweat broke out on my forehead as I thought of what Heather had told me.

"A woman drowned."

I gasped, "Was it Magda McCloud?"

The cop looked at me with surprise and twisting around, spoke into his walkie talkie. Turning back to me, he said, "Ma'am, go on. An officer will meet you for a statement. What is your camp site number?"

"I'm in the back row next to the river. Tell him to look for my turquoise VW. Can't miss it."

The policeman relayed the information to whoever was listening on the other end. "Okay. Go directly to your spot and don't leave. Give me a moment to move my vehicle."

I waited for the police car to move and then drove into the campgrounds. There were cop cars everywhere, many still flashing their lights. I could see paramedics moving a body to the back of an ambulance resting by the banks of the Kentucky River. I pulled into my spot and rushed over to Shaneika's RV. "Hello? Hello," I called out, but the RV was empty. Obviously, Shaneika and Heather were speaking to the police. I went back to my van, retrieved my binoculars, and let Baby out.

"Baby, stay with me," I commanded, after giving

him a chew toy. He took the toy and sat in the shade of a tree, gnawing happily. I turned my attention to the goings-on. I knew Baby was safely enraptured with his toy and wouldn't budge.

Oh, Lordy, why didn't I take Heather's alarm more seriously! Poor Magda Dane McCloud. Heather wasn't able to warn her in time. I watched the commotion through the binoculars and saw Shaneika speaking with a state trooper. She seemed very upset. I saw Shaneika glance at the RV. I waved my arm so she could see I was back. She returned my signal as both she and the trooper began walking toward me. "Come Baby. Come." Baby, clutching his toy, and I climbed into the RV to wait for Shaneika and the policewoman.

After several minutes, Shaneika and a trooper entered the RV. I was stunned at how upset Shaneika looked. She was crying.

"Shaneika! Whatever is the matter? You can't be that broken hearted over Magda McCloud's death. It's a tragedy for sure, but it's a shock to see you so shook up."

Shaneika looked at me through tear-stained eyes. "Josiah, it's not Magda McCloud. It's Heather. Heather is dead!"

6

Stunned, I fell onto the couch.

Knowing something was wrong, Baby dropped his toy and came over, putting his head in my lap, looking wistfully at me with his one good eye.

I asked, "What happened?"

Shaneika sat on the couch with me. "Heather was found this morning floating in the river." We both looked up and glimpsed at the ambulance passing by the open door of the RV.

"Is that Heather?" I asked.

Shaneika nodded.

The Kentucky State Trooper still standing, said, "Ma'am, I need to ask you a few questions. I'll make it fast and then I'll be on my way."

Shaneika said, "This is Sergeant Trimble. She's with the Kentucky State Police."

"Oh, yes," I mumbled. "This is state property. I didn't even notice the Kentucky State vehicles amongst the local police cars." I started hyperventilating. "I'm sorry. I need a moment. This is quite a shock." I took my asthma spray from my work apron pocket, which I was still wearing and took a hit, breathing deeply. "Give me a moment, please. This news is taking the wind right out of my sails."

"Mrs. Reynolds, I need to talk with you. You asked the guard at the entrance if Magda McCloud was dead. Why would you think that?"

I took a drink of stale water left on the end table and took another hit of my asthma spray. I inhaled deeply, trying to catch my breath.

Baby whimpered in sympathy.

I petted him. "It's okay, Baby. I'm fine." Looking up at the trooper, I said, "Please sit down. I don't like cops hovering over me."

"Thank you." The trooper sat beside me. "My name is Sergeant Kate Trimble. Can you state your full name and address?"

I studied Trimble, who cut an imposing figure. She was wearing the standard gray uniform of the State Police—gray long sleeve shirt with a dark tie tucked into the pants. Underneath the shirt I could see a white crew-neck T-shirt which was standard wear. The pants were gray sporting a black stripe down each side. Her campaign hat with its brass seal attached to the front gave Trimble an air of authority—that and her Glock Model 17 9 mm she wore. I recognized the gun as it was similar to the one my daughter Asa, carried now and then. "I'm Josiah Louise Reynolds and live in the Butterfly on Tates Creek Road."

"What's your occupation?"

"Mainly, I'm a beekeeper. I own a farm on the Palisades."

Shaneika added, "She also co-owns a catering/rental business with my mother, Eunice Leticia Todd."

Trimble pushed back her hat and insisted, "I want to know why you assumed it was Magda Dane McCloud, who was deceased."

"Because of what Heather told me this morning."

Shaneika asked, "You saw Heather this morning?"

"Let me ask the questions please, Ms. Todd," reprimanded Sergeant Trimble. "You saw Heather Warfield this morning?"

I couldn't help but chuckle when I saw Shaneika give Trimble a withering stare. "Yes, around six this morning before I left for work."

"What did Heather say?" Shaneika asked.

"She told me she caught Magda's husband, Gavin, kissing her sister Maja, as they were discussing murdering Magda before Monday."

Writing furiously in her notebook, Trimble asked, "Who are they exactly?"

Shaneika chimed in, "They are Magda and Maja Dane—identical twin sisters of a very powerful and rich family from Baltimore. Magda Dane is married to Gavin McCloud. Magda told us yesterday that she had sold the family business without her siblings' knowledge. That's why the Dane family was having a family reunion here so Magda could tell them. She was afraid her sisters might not take it well even though they would make a pile of money."

"What are their names?"

"Her twin is Maja Dane. Her older sister is Margot Dane, and they had an older brother, but he is deceased."

Sergeant Trimble didn't reply, but kept writing. "Does Monday have any special significance?"

"That's when the transfer of ownership would take place," I said. "Look, how did Heather die?"

"We think she accidentally drowned, but we won't know for sure until the autopsy report."

Shaneika shook her head. "No, that woman did not drown. Heather would never get close to the river. She was afraid of large bodies of water."

I added, "Heather didn't know how to swim unless it was the dog paddle. She was a terrible swimmer." I pointed out toward the open door. "You talk to Maja and Gavin. That's where you'll find the answer to Heather's death. She caught two people planning murder, and they killed her for it."

"You say Heather was afraid of water, and yet, all three of you parked next to the river."

"Parking several hundred yards from the river and being in the river are two different things," I said. I could tell Sergeant Trimble thought I was being too sassy. I had to bring it down a notch. As a rule, law enforcement types didn't appreciate me.

"It's a rather fantastic story you are repeating, Mrs. Reynolds. That kind of thing only happens in the movies. I think we'll find that Miss Warfield went bird watching near the river, slipped, and fell in. If she didn't swim as you say, that makes it more plausible."

"Fantastic or not, you will talk to the Dane family?" I asked.

"Of course. We will leave no stone unturned." Sergeant Trimble put away her notebook and stood. She was a tall plain woman with a man's haircut and no makeup. Her only vanity was wearing a wedding ring. This woman was all business with a capital "B." "I will need a formal statement from both of you. Where will you both be in the next couple of days?"

I glanced at Shaneika. She gave a slight nod of her head. "I'm staying until the dig is finished."

"I am, too," Shaneika said.

Sergeant Trimble thrust her thumbs in her belt. "Ladies, I'm giving you warning. Leave this to the professionals."

"I don't know what you mean," I said innocently.

"Mrs. Reynolds, you have a reputation of meddling in police affairs. Your reputation precedes you."

"I'm sure you mean the murders that I have helped the police solve."

Trimble tipped her hat. "I'll be in touch for a formal statement after I check out both of your alibis. Right now, I need to interview everyone at the campground, and then I'll circle around to those I need to re-interview, but I definitely want to speak with you two again."

I stood. "Heather did not slip and fall into the river, and Ms. Todd and I had nothing to do with her death. Talk to the Danes. That's where you'll find the answers."

"If you leave the campgrounds, please notify me."

"Does that go for the Danes as well?"

"Yes, until the final say so from the medical examiner."

"When will the autopsy take place?"

"As soon as Miss Warfield's body reaches the morgue. It might be possible for an answer today."

Shaneika asked, "Has anyone officially identified the body and claimed it?"

"You declared she was Heather Warfield when we arrived. We will be notifying her family shortly."

"Heather is an only child. Her parents live in Florida. I'll come down later this afternoon and handle the paperwork for the transfer of her body to the funeral home," Shaneika said.

"Do you have that right?"

"I am Heather's lawyer and will handle her estate. Her parents are elderly. I don't want to put them through unnecessary trauma. I'll be by later."

"Suit yourself. Thank you for your time, ladies. I'll be seeing you again," Sergeant Trimble said as she exited the RV.

Shaneika closed the door and said, "You want to start from the top?"

"Yeah, then let's hang out front. I want to see how the Danes act."

"I need a drink," Shaneika said. "You want one?"

"No, thanks. I want to keep my head clear."

"That's a first."

"What does that mean?"

"Nothing," Shaneika said, pouring bourbon into a cup.

I didn't reply for I knew Shaneika was angry with me. I don't know how Heather got herself killed after I told her to stay inside the RV, but why, oh why, didn't I take her with me to the market!

I just didn't think of it. Maybe my mind is fuzzy from all the pain medication and the bourbon.

I now regret not taking Heather with me.

I so regret it.

7

It took a couple of hours for Heather's death to sink in. I sat in front of my van with Baby, watching the police cars leave, one by one, as life went on. The police were getting calls for other emergencies and were needed elsewhere. The archaeological volunteers drifted back to the dig as the archaeologists pulled back the tarps to continue working. Kayaks glided past on the river like swans. Several new campers pulled into spots with their RVs. Noisy children ran and played, but the atmosphere in the camp was different—hesitant, furtive, and uneasy. Everyone, who had worked on the dig, was shaken up, and that was most of us still at the campgrounds.

One of the archaeologists named Rebecca, whom we called Becky, walked over and expressed her condolences. She told me she was the one who found Heather in the water and notified the camp manager. The woman was upset, but offered to show me exactly where she found Heather's body. I grabbed my ebony cane, topped with a silver wolf's head, and walked with her to the river's edge. It was a precarious walk for me, but I didn't care. It was the least I could do. Baby lumbered behind us sniffing trees every few feet.

"There," Becky said, pointing.

"Why were you down here? The dig is yards away."

"It was early morning and the mist was still on the river. It was so beautiful I wanted to take a picture."

"Were other people up?"

"Just a few but nobody was by the river. Just me."

"What time was that?"

"Almost seven, but not quite."

I said, "I left about six fifteen after I talked to Heather."

"I didn't know anyone had spoken with her."

"Yeah, I did."

In a small voice, Becky said, "Oh, I see." She shifted the weight on her feet.

I said, "You said you saw several people up and about. Did you know who they were?"

"I saw the Carpenters. They were taking their dogs out for a quick run."

"They are the older couple working on the dig?"

"Yes, they headed over to the pool area."

I asked, "Anyone else? How about the Danes?"

"I saw someone go into their RV, but I couldn't tell you who it was as she was wearing a hoodie."

"You said she. You believe it was a woman?"

"I would say a woman as the figure was slight."

Noting that I stood taller, I sized up Becky's figure. She was petite like the Dane twins. "Are the Dane sisters still going to work on the dig?"

"Yes, in fact, Magda and Maja's sibling will be joining us today. I understand they are having a family reunion." Becky wrung her hands. "I don't even want to continue the dig, but we must in order to comply with the grant terms. The park wants us to finish by eight on Sunday night."

"Becky, don't feel guilty about the dig."

The archeologist looked gratefully at me.

"Did you know Heather well?"

"She was a member of the Boone Archaeological Society. She had worked with me on several digs. We were friendly but not close. I thought she was a sweet woman."

"I see. One more thing."

"Yes?"

"You're staying in the campgrounds, Becky?"

"I'm three spots away from you."

"That's what I thought. Did you hear or see anything unusual this morning before you found Heather?"

"I heard you leave. Your van has a distinctive putt putt."

"Did I wake you?"

"No, I was awake before that."

"Nothing odd?"

"Nothing. I'm sorry, Josiah. I really am. This is a dreadful business."

I nodded.

"Look, I've got to get back." Becky looked toward the dig.

"Sure."

She clasped my hand. "Let me know if you need anything."

"I will. Thank you. I certainly appreciate speaking with you."

While Becky walked back to the site, I checked the river bank looking for marks where Heather could have fallen into the river.

"Find anything?"

I looked up to see Shaneika extending a disposable coffee cup to me.

"The food truck finally got here."

"Thanks," I said, taking the coffee. I sniffed it.

"It's tea. I know you're not a fan of coffee."

"I'm grateful," I replied, before taking a sip.

"Whatcha doing?"

"Looking to see if there were signs where Heather might have slipped and fallen into the water."

"Find anything?"

"Nada."

"I didn't see anything either."

I mused, "You'd think with the ground being wet,

we'd find footprints of some sorts."

"Maybe Heather was on the beach?"

"Let's check," I said.

The beach was a man-made sandy beach next to Lock 10 at the park. It was created when people were still allowed to swim in the Kentucky River, before E. coli was discovered in the water. The park built a pool and forbade swimming in the river. The beach had since eroded into a small sliver of what was once its former glory. It was a shame as the river was so beautiful, but people, up and down the river, still dump their sewage illegally into the river, and officials do nothing about it.

Little had changed since the Boonesborough pioneers settled this spot. They also dumped their waste and garbage into the river and their privies leached into the water as well. It was noted in many pioneer journals that one could smell Fort Boonesborough before one saw it. And we're not talking about the sweet smells of flowers.

Shaneika and I ambled to the beach and found it covered with debris from the river. Nothing seemed out of place except for lots of footprints belonging to the police. Baby ran ahead, chasing birds away. I took out my phone and snapped away at the beach and surrounding area.

"There's nothing here," I said. "I don't think Heather came this way or else her body would have drifted toward the lock."

"The police said Heather was snagged on some driftwood."

"Let's go back," I suggested.

"Okay. There's nothing to see here, anyway."

As we were trudging up a little incline, Magda and Maja Dane intercepted us.

"Hello," they both said in unison.

Baby immediately pushed his way in front and whimpered, stretching out his neck to sniff the women. As soon as Baby smelled the woman on the left, he wagged his tail.

"Hello, Magda," I said to the woman on the left wearing a checkered blue and white wool scarf with her navy pea coat.

Magda laughed as she petted Baby. "Ah, he remembers me."

Wearing a red parka with a geometric red and orange scarf, Maja said, "We just wanted to tell you how sorry we are about the death of your friend." Annoyed, she pushed Baby away when he sniffed her.

"Come here, Baby. My little sister doesn't care for fur babies," Magda said, loving on Baby again while Maja looked irritated.

Shaneika started to reply to Maja, but I gave her a small nudge.

"Thank you, Maja," I replied. "Heather's death has been quite a shock."

"Was it suicide?" Maja asked.

"No, absolutely not," Shaneika answered, heatedly.

"The police are still determining whether it was an accident or murder," I said.

"Murder?" Magda said, looking alarmed.

I said, "It's a possibility, especially after what Heather told me she saw this morning."

"What was that?" Maja asked.

"How was your family reunion?" I asked the twins, trying to catch them off guard.

Maja answered, "It was great to see our sister. We hadn't seen her in years."

"Just wondering if any unexpected announcements were made last night."

Maja shot a glance at Magda, who looked unperturbed at our questioning. "What are you getting at?"

"Did you all stay at the hotel last night?" Shaneika asked, ignoring Maja's question.

"Why do you want to know?" Maja asked.

I said to Magda, "Just curious. There's a witness who said she saw a hooded female enter your RV around the time Heather died."

"That wasn't us. Gavin and Magda stayed over at the B&B with Margot and me," Maja said. "We didn't get here until nine. Heather's body had already been discovered by that time."

"I visited the RV this morning," Magda said. "It was locked up tight as a drum, and nothing was disturbed."

"You two and Gavin come in the same car?" I asked.

Shifting her feet uneasily, Maja said, "We're sorry for your loss. Come on, Magda. We need to get back."

"Yes, we do." Magda smiled, and after giving Baby one last pat, followed Maja.

Shaneika and I waited until they were out of earshot to speak.

"They are two creepy gals," Shaneika said. "What do you think?"

"I think they are lying through their teeth."

"That's what my gut tells me as well. I think they were fishing for information."

"Let's see what they do with the bait about Heather telling me something."

"If you turn up dead as well, then I'll know Heather really did see Gavin and Maja planning Magda's murder."

"Thanks, pal. I agree that Heather did see and hear something that got her killed, but what?"

Shaneika said, "Don't you think it strange that Magda seems passive around Gavin and Maja, yet she is the boss of a billion dollar company controlling their money."

"I think it's for show. Perhaps she is a tiger in her professional life, but prefers her family to take care of the personal end of things."

"That's why you pay a housekeeper and a personal assistant."

I said, "I don't think Magda has many friends she can trust. That kind of lifestyle dictates business partners, acquaintances, employees, and colleagues. Very few close friends. I think she would be jealous of our circle of friends."

Shaneika's phone rang and she answered, "Yes. Yes. Okay. We'll be there soon. We're coming now."

"Who's that?"

"Sergeant Trimble. She wants to see us in her office. I think something has turned up."

"Did she say what?"

"No, but let's take your van."

"Where's Trimble's office?"

"She's at Post 7 in Richmond. Let's hurry."

I gave Shaneika my keys, so she could go ahead and start the vehicle. Baby went with her, leaving me to struggle up the small incline. I kept looking behind me as I didn't want the Dane twins to circle around and jump me from behind. Yes, I was being paranoid. Wouldn't be the first time.

I knew I had hit a tender spot. Their answers didn't jive with what Magda told us yesterday and with Heather's story this morning.

One thing was sure—the twins had decided to join forces and cover for each other.

It seemed that blood was thicker than river water.

8

"Thank you for coming promptly. I wanted to get your official statements before the day ended," Sergeant Trimble said, beckoning to chairs on the other side of the table on which sat a tape recorder. "I would like to interview you two separately."

"That's not going to happen," I replied. "I make it a rule not to talk with law enforcement without my lawyer present, and my lawyer is Ms. Todd. That is my right as an American citizen."

Trimble looked perturbed, but said, "If you insist."

"I do."

"Then be seated, please."

Shaneika and I sat down.

Trimble turned on the tape recorder and motioned for someone to turn on the video camera stationed in the upper right corner of the room. She stated her name with the date and time and asked us to identify ourselves as well.

"Has something happened?" Shaneika asked.

"Miss Warfield's autopsy is not yet complete, but the medial examiner sent these pictures over an hour ago. I would like to have your opinion on them." Trimble shoved two 8x10 glossy photographs toward us.

Shaneika and I picked up one each and perused them. I felt squeamish doing so. Then we traded pictures and studied them intently.

"Well?" Trimble asked.

I said, "There are two reddish marks spaced approximately two inches or less apart. I would say this picture is of Heather's neck area. There are another two marks that look similar on her back left shoulder."

I tossed my picture onto the table. "They are stun gun marks. Heather was hit with a Taser or a stun gun or both."

Trimble gathered the photos and inserted them into a file. "That's what the medical examiner and I think."

I said, "So Heather was rendered helpless and thrown into the river to drown."

"The medical examiner thinks Miss Warfield was dead before she hit the water," Trimble said.

"What?" Shaneika gasped.

"Heather Warfield died of heart failure brought on by being tased."

"In other words, she died of shock," Shaneika said.

"It looks to me that she was tased by two different stun guns," I said.

"My thoughts as well," Sergeant Trimble said. She brushed back a stray hair. "Do either of you own a stun gun?"

"I do," I said, pulling it out of my purse. I handed it over to Trimble.

She handed it back after examining it, saying, "The prongs on this one are different from the one used on Miss Warfield. What about you, Ms. Todd?"

"I don't own one."

"Would you mind if one of my troopers examined your RV?"

"You don't think we had anything to do with this, do you?" Shaneika asked, incredulous.

"I told you to interview the Dane twins!" I said. "Those two women had something to do with Heather's death."

"We did, and they, as well as the husband, have solid alibis."

I said, "They are covering up for one another, but Heather said she saw Maja and Gavin in the woods, plotting to kill Magda."

"Here's the problem I have with this story—how did Miss Warfield know it was Maja and not Magda? I can't tell those two apart close up, so how did Miss Warfield standing some distance away?"

"Because Heather said she heard them say 'to kill her before Monday.' That's when the sale of the business was to finalize," I replied.

"Miss Warfield used the word 'kill?'"

I thought for a moment. "Well, not exactly, but that's what she meant. Murder was implied."

"Ms. Todd?"

Shaneika shook her head. "As per my original statement, I never talked to Heather. I didn't know something had happened to her until someone fetched me."

"Who was that?"

Shaneika sighed. "The camp manager. He had been notified by some early kayakers."

"You never spoke with Heather?" I asked, astonished.

Shaneika turned to me. "No. I didn't see her. I never spoke with her."

"That explains a lot," I said. "I told Heather to stay in the RV and speak with you before she did anything. You were still asleep."

"The camp manager woke me up."

"Do you think the twins busted into the RV and kidnapped Heather?" I asked Trimble.

"That is one of the reasons we want to search your RV, Ms. Todd. It may be a crime scene."

"Then you have my permission, but nothing looked disturbed this morning. I will be present when you search it."

"But we have your permission?"

"Yes. You won't need a warrant. I want you to

65

catch whoever did this to Heather."

"What about your car, Mrs. Reynolds?"

"My van is sitting in the parking lot now. Your boys can go over it as soon as we finish with this interview, and I am present." Pausing for a moment, I asked, "You said the camp manager said kayakers discovered Heather's body?"

Trimble said, "Yes."

"One of the archaeologists told me that she discovered Heather's body," I said.

"Who was that?" Trimble asked.

"Her first name is Rebecca. I don't know her last name. We all call her Becky," I replied. "She said she notified the camp manager."

"I'd like to talk with her," Trimble said, writing the woman's name down. "Very good. Let's go on to something else." Trimble pulled out a set of keys and placed them on the table. "Do either one of you recognize these keys?"

Shaneika picked them up and said, "They are Heather's. All items like sunglasses, pens, keys had UK's decals on them. She was a huge basketball fan."

"Is that where she went to school?"

"No, she went out-of-state up north to an ivy-league school. Where did you find them?"

"On the ground between your RV and her car."

Shaneika and I glanced at each other.

"Heather must have decided to leave and was attacked beside her car. Did you find her purse?" I asked.

"No."

"Did you use luminol in her car?" Shaneika asked.

"Yes, but nothing." Trimble tapped her finger on the table. "Why was her car parked in the spot next to your RV, Ms. Todd?"

I answered, "The three of us came separately on Thursday. Heather and I both paid for spots to park our cars on either side of the RV where we slept. This saved driving time to and from Lexington."

"Whose RV is it?"

"It's mine," Shaneika said. "It's a rental from a former client."

"Why didn't Miss Warfield come with either one of you?"

"She lived in the other direction from Mrs. Reynolds or me," Shaneika said.

Trimble said, "I see." She thought for a moment. "Ms. Todd, I understand that you and Heather Warfield were related."

"Our ancestors were the first Europeans and African Americans to come to this area."

"And you are related to Miss Warfield how?"

"The Warfields and the Todds have common ancestors. All of the original families from the 1700s intermarried with each other, and the white men dallied with their slaves. Heather and I took DNA tests, and we have common ancestors both male and female. We had been working together to find out the female lines of descent."

"Any blood feuds between the families?"

Shaneika laughed. "You are not from around here, are you? If you were, you wouldn't be asking such a foolish question. We are not the Hatfields and the McCoys."

"Any racial issues between you and Heather Warfield? As you said, the white men took advantage of their female slaves."

Shaneika stiffened. "Are you asking because I'm black?"

"Frankly, yes."

"White and black people in this area have come to terms with our history and embraced it—both good and bad. We just want to move forward."

Trimble replied, "Sounds very noble, but it usually doesn't work that way. As William Faulkner said, 'The past is never dead. It's not even past.'"

"I don't know what you expect me to say. Heather and I were family."

Not satisfied with Shaneika's answer, Trimble addressed the same issue but in a more roundabout way. "Did you ever experience prejudice from Miss Warfield which made you angry?"

"Heather and I were on very good terms. I enjoyed her company. We were both interested in history, especially Kentucky history. Historians say that St.

Louis was the gateway to the West. It wasn't. It was Kentucky. As for prejudice? Sure, I've experienced it and still do occasionally, but so do fat people, gay people, disabled people, and the elderly—the world is full of prejudice. The Bluegrass has always been pretty tolerant though. That is until outsiders started moving here."

Since Sergeant Trimble had a New Jersey accent, she sniffed at the last remark which was obviously aimed at her. She directed her ire at me. "Did you believe what Miss Warfield told you?"

"Yes, I believe she saw and heard something which frightened her."

"And yet, you did nothing about it."

Guilt came rushing over me. "I regret it so much. I was late for work and wanted to deal with it when I got back. I told Heather to stay locked in the RV and tell Shaneika when she woke up. As an attorney, she would know the best way to proceed."

"You're saying Heather's death is my fault?" Shaneika snapped.

"NO! No. Not that. I never thought anything would happen. People were rising for the morning, so I thought she was safe. I sincerely regret that I didn't take Heather with me. Oh, how I regret it!" Tears formed in my eyes as I searched in my purse for a hanky.

"Why wouldn't Miss Warfield wake you up if she

was that frightened, Ms. Todd?" Trimble asked.

"I had complained of being tired the evening before. Heather was allowing me to sleep in. She was considerate that way." Shaneika leaned forward and said, "Something happened to make Heather bolt. She was a shy, timid person. She never would have confronted Gavin McCloud or the Dane twins on her own. Did you examine her phone?"

"We can't find that either." Trimble made some notes on a legal pad. "Was the door of your RV locked when you awoke, Ms. Todd?"

"I don't remember. I got up to answer the door, and everything is pretty much a blur after that."

I said, encouragingly, "Think Shaneika. When the camp manager came for you, did you unlock the door or just swing it open?"

"Josiah, I don't remember."

I could tell Shaneika's nerves were on edge. I had never seen her rattled, but then her cousin hadn't been murdered before.

"Did you notice any damage to the door or anything upset in the RV?" Sergeant Trimble asked.

Shaneika shook her head. "I threw on some clothes and ran to the river. I didn't look at anything in the RV."

I asked, "Did you lock the RV door when you left?"

"I'm asking the questions here, Mrs. Reynolds."

"Ask them, Sergeant."

"Did you lock the RV door when you left, Ms. Todd?" Trimble asked.

"Geez," I mumbled.

Trimble shot me a stern look.

I was starting to get the shakes. I hadn't eaten and my leg was throbbing. I needed to switch out my pain patch. I was beginning to wonder if throwing out all my black market pain medication was a good idea, but I was becoming a junkie. I had to break the cycle, but I was hurting bad now. Unless a person suffers from chronic pain, they have no idea how constant hurting can send a person off the deep end. The depression that goes along with pill addiction is just as nasty as the actual addiction.

Noticing my pale and shaky countenance, Shaneika stepped up the interview. "Are you declaring Heather's death a homicide?"

"We will be waiting for the medical examiner's final report, but it looks that way."

Shaneika stood and pulled me up with her. "Will you have one of your men drive us back to the campsite? You may keep Mrs. Reynolds van for your forensic guys, but right now, Mrs. Reynolds is in need of a meal and her meds. We didn't expect this interview to take so long. We can pick the van up tomorrow if you leave it in the parking lot."

Trimble stood in alarm, noticing my pale and sweating appearance. "Mrs. Reynolds, you don't look well."

"I don't feel well. I had an accident several years ago, and my body has never fully recovered."

"I'm very sorry. What happened?"

"I was pulled off a cliff by a crazy cop and hit a rock outcrop forty feet below, which was a blessing as the cliff was eighty feet high. The cop is now dead. Murdered."

Sergeant Trimble's eyes narrowed.

That was the end of the interview as we were shown the door.

9

It seemed Trimble changed her mind about inspecting my van, but still wanted to inspect the RV. We followed her forensic team to the campsite. Of course, Baby rushed them barking and growling when the forensic team opened the RV door. I think one trooper tinkled in her pants—just a tad. Another called me a naughty word for not warning them.

I shrugged. I know I'm a stinker. I should have warned them about my two hundred and twenty pound Mastiff, but what's the point? There is no use telling people that Baby's bark is worse than his bite. People never believe me, so why bother. Baby pushed by them when I called his name and stood beside me.

While Shaneika pulled up a chair and waited outside the RV, I took Baby on a tinkle walk as we drifted over to the archaeological site. They were closing shop for the night. I called out to the volunteers, "Find anything interesting today?"

Becky yelled back, "Same old. Same old."

"Lots of animal bones. Broken pottery. That sort of thing. Nothing earthshaking," another volunteer called out.

One of the archaeologists named Ellison Brody came over to me. He was tall, dark, and hunky with a pretty boy face and killer body. Yes, Ellison was nice on the eyes. I forgot about my leg pain. After petting Baby, he said, "Actually, from today's haul, we can pinpoint the pioneers' diet and what goods they brought with them."

"Don't we already know what they ate from their diaries? They ate wild meat. Within two years the first wave of settlers hunted all the game out of the area. And they grew corn."

"We think we know. This will pinpoint their diet precisely."

"I see."

"Will you be coming tomorrow?"

"I'll be on the dig bright and early."

"Dr. Reese got a call this afternoon informing her that everyone on the dig is not to leave until Sunday night. The Kentucky State Troopers are doing another round of interviews tomorrow. Know why?"

"Can they do that?"

Ellison shrugged. "Don't know. I guess people could push at it, but why? It would just draw attention to oneself and make the police suspicious."

"I guess they just want to be sure about Heather's

death. Making sure no foul play was involved." I didn't want people to know yet that Heather's death was suspicious. It gave the police an edge to find the culprit.

"A tragedy for sure. I haven't told you how sorry I am. She was such a nice lady."

"Did you know Heather well?"

"Just worked with her several times. Heather loved history."

"Yes, she loved history," I repeated. "Let me ask you something."

"Sure."

"You worked with Heather on several digs."

"Yeah, we loved having her. Heather was a good worker. Never complained."

"Was there anyone she had trouble with on one of these digs?"

"What do you mean?"

"A man giving her unwanted attention or someone with whom she argued? Someone who irritated her. You know—someone she didn't get on with."

"I don't think so. Heather got on with everyone."

"Did she have any special friends?"

"Heather would go for beers with the archaeologists after work. You know, to relax, but as for a special friend, I don't think so. I can't seem to think of anyone but Shaneika Todd. They would always work together."

Disappointed, I said, "I see."

"Is there a problem? Heather drowned, didn't she?

It was an accident, I assumed."

"Most probably. I was just wondering."

"I know she wasn't a good swimmer."

"No, she wasn't, so why was she down by the river?"

Ellison gave me an odd look. "People are saying she was bird watching and slipped, falling into the river. Binoculars were found around her neck."

"Yep, that's what people are saying."

"What's going on at Shaneika's RV?"

"A forensic team is checking for any evidence that might explain Heather's demise."

Ellison seemed perplexed. "I don't understand. She drowned. Right?"

"The State Police are just being thorough. Standard procedure."

Ellison looked at me as though he didn't believe my reasoning, but he decided not to push it. "Let me know if there is anything the archeology team can do in this time of grief."

"Will do. Thank you."

Impatient to be off, Ellison said, "I've got to help my wife, so I'll see you tomorrow."

Oh, darn, Ellison was married.

"I'll be here," I replied, wondering who his wife was. As I watched Ellison walk away, I chuckled a bit. If my heart rate was checked this very moment, it would cause the doctor alarm, as I could feel my heart thumping rapidly. I so liked a handsome chap, and it felt good that a man still could make my blood race. It meant I was alive and still in the game, pain be damned. It made me wish for Hunter and long for the day he would come home. He had been away a month now, and I was missing him more than I thought I would. Maybe I would marry him. I wondered if Heather had a beau.

I continued my walk and wandered over to where Becky was washing mud off the tools. "Hi, Becky."

"Oh, hi Josiah. Hi Baby."

Baby wagged his tail and looked at her hopefully for a treat.

I asked, "May I help you?"

"Sure. You dry these off and store them away in these tubs."

"No problem." I grabbed some paper towels and dried off brushes, trowels, and other tools of the archeology trade. After a few moments, I asked, "Becky, did you see any kayaks on the river when you found Heather this morning?"

"I don't know what you mean."

"Was anyone kayaking on the river when you found Heather?"

Becky seemed to hesitate. "I don't recall."

"Anyone else around?"

"People were starting to stir, but no one was around the river banks. Why?"

"Did you pull Heather out of the water?"

"No, the bank is rather steep there. I needed help, so I went to find the camp manager."

"And he didn't know about Heather until you told him."

"Of course not. Hey, what are you getting at?"

"Nothing. I'm just trying to fit the pieces together. That's all. Hand me those trowels, and I'll dry them off for you."

Becky and I didn't speak for the rest of the time we worked and when finished, we bade each other good night, going our separate ways. By the time I got back to Shaneika's RV, the forensic team was packing up.

I found Shaneika inspecting the RV. "Did they find anything?"

"They sprayed luminol looking for blood and checked for fingerprints. I'm hoping they'll find prints other than ours on the door."

"Did they find any blood?"

"Some, but this is a rented RV. It could be any-one's."

"Where did they find it?"

"In the most likely areas—the kitchen and bath-room areas. Nothing by the door."

"What if someone knocked on the door, misidenti-fied himself, and pulled Heather from the RV when she opened the door."

"That's a theory."

I asked, "Who would Heather open the door for?"

Shaneika thought for a moment. "The camp manager or either one of the archaeologists."

"Speaking of archaeologists, Ellison stopped me to give his condolences. He was very curious as to why the troopers were in your RV."

Shaneika pressed her lips together.

"He said he had to help his wife. Who's his wife?"

"Dr. Reese."

"Dr. Allison Reese? She's his wife? They have different last names."

"His last name is Brody."

"Tell me something I don't know."

Shaneika pulled a soft drink out of the fridge. "Want one?"

I plopped down on the couch. "Naw. Tell me more about Ellison and Dr. Reese. Why don't we call Ellison doctor?"

"Because he's not one. He just finished his Masters in plant biology. He specializes in dating plant matter."

"He seems to be quite a bit younger than Dr. Reese, and I must say, shyer and more reserved."

"Well, it's the typical teacher and student scenario. You know how those things go."

"Yeah, usually with a lawsuit and someone getting fired."

"Ellison is in his early thirties, well beyond the age of consent."

"How long have they been a couple?"

Shaneika thought for a moment. "I think Heather told me they had been married for four years."

"Hmm, they hooked up when Ellison was in his late twenties. Good for Dr. Reese. Who doesn't want a bit of arm candy, and Ellison is very handsome."

"Quit making their relationship sound salacious. It is nothing of the sort with Dr. Reese," Shaneika said, heatedly.

I looked intently at my friend, as she nervously avoided eye contact. I have known Shaneika long enough to recognize when she is being deceitful. After all, she is my daughter's age and I am a mom. Mothers can smell a lie a mile away. "What's going on, Shaneika? Is there something you're not telling me?"

She remained silent.

"How did Heather know that Ellison Brody and Dr. Reese had been married for four years? I didn't even know they were related, and I bet you most of the people on this dig don't know they are married. They arrive and leave in separate cars, going in separate directions when they pull out of the campgrounds."

"They are taking a break from their marriage."

"And how do you know that?"

Shaneika poured bourbon into her soft drink, ignoring me.

"Shaneika?"

"Let's go into town for dinner," she said.

"Shaneika, answer me. You're not great friends with Ellison or Dr. Reese, so how do you know that?"

"I guess it doesn't matter now that Heather is dead. She had an affair with Ellison, and Dr. Reese found out about it."

"What! Our shy, timid Heather had an affair with heartthrob Ellison! I don't believe you. I mean I believe you, but I'm shocked. Yes, really surprised."

"Heather confided in me last year. It had been going on for some time, and Dr. Reese caught them, demanding that Ellison not see Heather anymore."

"Which he did," I stated as a fact, rather than a question.

"Yes, but I couldn't get through to Heather that she needed to let go. She was obsessed with Ellison. When I found out Heather was determined to come on this dig, I tried to stop her."

"So we came along as chaperones to keep her out of trouble."

Shaneika nodded. "I'm sorry I didn't tell you, Josiah, but I promised to keep this affair quiet, especially after Dr. Reese threatened Heather with a restraining order after she saw her on Thursday."

"You must have handled it."

"I broached a deal with Dr. Reese to allow Heather to continue on the excavation, as long as Heather stayed away from Ellison. If she were caught having contact with him, Dr. Reese would file a restraining order."

"That's a tenuous deal at best. It explains why Dr. Reese came over to our lunch table. She was warning Heather to keep to the deal. That tempest speech and all."

"I couldn't make Heather leave the field, so to speak, and I didn't want Dr. Reese calling the police, so it was the best compromise I could make."

"What did Ellison say about the deal?"

"He was never consulted. I talked with Dr. Reese only."

"Did you believe Heather would hold up her end of the bargain?"

Shaneika shook her head. "I didn't believe Heather had the discipline to stay away from Ellison."

"Did Ellison still have the hots for Heather?"

"I don't know, but he did cut off all communication with Heather after Dr. Reese demanded it of him last year, even after he and Dr. Reese separated. He refused phone calls, letters, blocked her from facebook—everything. He cut her dead."

I said, "That's a poor phrase of words there."

"Let's not attack each other. It hardly foments a partnership to discovering Heather's murderer."

"Point taken," I said. "Let's think outside the box. Maybe it was Heather who was sneaking off to see Ellison this morning? Maybe Ellison was secretly seeing Heather, and she threatened to expose him this weekend? Maybe she wanted Ellison to declare his freedom from Dr. Reese?"

"I've been wondering about that. It crossed my mind that she was meeting Ellison and they saw you. She made up that story about the Danes to pull you away because she didn't want you to see him."

"Plausible. She seemed really frightened to me though. I think I would have detected if she was deceiving me."

"Like you did about her having a salacious love affair?"

"You got me there. Didn't see that coming at all."

"Are you angry with me?" Shaneika asked.

"Yeah, but I'll get over it."

"I'm so sorry to have dragged you into this."

"Have you told Trimble?"

"Yes, this morning. It's one of the reasons she wants to interview everyone again. What do you think?"

"At the moment I'm hungry and exhausted, not to mention confused. I have to have a think."

"Let's go into town. There is a nice Chinese restaurant in the mall. Take us fifteen minutes to get there."

"Do they serve liquor?"

"Yes."

"Then I'm your gal." I threw my keys at her. "You drive."

After I put on a fresh pain patch, we locked the RV up tight with Baby inside and went to get something to eat. I was always hesitant to leave Baby alone in a car in a public parking area for a period of time, afraid due to the probability someone might steal him. That's why I didn't take him.

I should have realized I was making the same mistake I had made with Heather.

10

We had a delicious supper while plying ourselves with hot tea and whiskey sodas. Both of us had calmed down considerably. I guess we had finally accepted Heather's death. Before it had been such a fright. We discussed several possible theories to explain Heather's death.

I said, "We need to find out who discovered Heather's body. I've heard two different versions so far. Becky said she found Heather, and Trimble said kayakers discovered the body."

"I think it is most likely kayakers discovered Heather. Sometimes people like to insert themselves in a tragedy to gain attention. We can ask for a clarification tomorrow," Shaneika said.

"From whom?"

"Trimble is the most obvious choice. I think we should check with the camp manager as well."

I asked, "Do you know Becky well?"

"She's a history buff like myself, but I always found

her pleasant enough. Other than seeing her and waving hello at university lectures and digs, I don't have any contact with her."

"I thought she was a bona fide archeologist."

"She is but never a shining star. Stays in the shadows. She'd be pretty if she combed her hair once in a while."

"This from a woman who has a different hairstyle every time I see her."

Shaneika said, "A woman should change her hairdo like she changes her purse. I suppose you wouldn't understand. You've had the same hairstyle since I've known you."

"Let's get back to Becky. What else do you know about her?"

"Nothing. She does her job. Becky is competent. She's a hard worker, but she's not a favorite with Dr. Reese."

"Why is that?"

Shaneika shrugged. "Don't know."

"They have a fight?"

"No. No. I don't think that's it. Sometimes I catch Becky staring at Dr. Reese, and it's not a friendly stare."

I asked, "How do you mean?"

"It's like she's studying Dr. Reese."

"That's a compliment."

Shaneika said, "Or it can be odd. I can't put my finger on it, but there's something off with Becky. She's bright and enthusiastic. Still, I feel on guard around her."

"Is she with someone?" I asked.

"I never noticed. Becky never really crossed my radar. Personally, I doubt that she'll ever make tenure. She doesn't publish enough."

I asked, "What do you think of Sergeant Trimble?"

"I think she is an ambitious detective who is bucking to make lieutenant. If Trimble doesn't crack this case by tomorrow night, I think she will be taken off it and it will be given to a more seasoned detective."

"It hasn't even been twenty-four hours yet. How much can Trimble get done in less than a day?"

"I think she's amassed an amazing amount of information in a short time."

I asked, "You think she's capable?"

"Yeah, I do," Shaneika said, motioning to the waitress.

"Let's look at the suspects," I said, dipping my egg roll into a bowl of sweet and sour sauce.

"Who's first on your list?"

"Well, I think Ellison is now. Both he and his wife have motive and opportunity. I don't think Heather would have opened the RV door for either of the Danes."

Shaneika said, "If Heather lied about breaking it off with Ellison, I think Dr. Reese is the prime suspect. Jealousy is a powerful motivator in a lot of murders.

I've tried enough of them in court."

"Heather was tased with a stun gun. I can't see Dr. Reese and Ellison working in concert to kill Heather over an affair."

"You've just refuted your own theory."

"I have, haven't I?" I said, pouring tea in both of our cups.

"That puts us back at the Dane twins or one of the twins working with Gavin."

"There's something very bizarre there. I don't care for them."

"The third sister worked at the dig today."

"The one from Martha's Vineyard?"

"Yeah. I sure would like to talk with her."

"I'd like to see if Magda told her two sisters about the family business being sold."

Giving up on chopsticks and picking up a fork, Shaneika said, "We'll see if the Dane twins fly in on their broomsticks tomorrow."

"If they are staying in town again, why don't we have a look-see in Gavin and Magda's RV tonight? We might find Heather's purse or phone."

"You'll have to do it, Josiah. I'm an officer of the court. I can't be breaking and entering. I'll lose my license."

I said, "Okay. Let's put together a plan of action. I'm going to sneak into the Magda Dane's RV. See if I find anything."

"If you do, the evidence won't be admissible in court."

I smiled. "I'll use the phone from the camp store to call the State Police and leave an anonymous tip if I find something interesting."

"Which any good lawyer will have thrown out of court because it looks like a setup."

I slumped back in my seat. "I know. I know. I'm grasping at straws. It feels wrong to have a nice meal while Heather is lying in a cold morgue."

Shaneika gave me her "let-the-professionals-handle-it" look.

"Okay. We'll play it by the book," I said, motioning to the waitress for more napkins. We finished our meal in silence, wondering what steps were needed next. I paid for the meal twenty minutes later and followed Shaneika to the van without resolving anything. It was just as well as I was exhausted, and my emotions were raw.

Shaneika drove back to the campground as I fell asleep in my seat with my head nodding on my chest. Suddenly, I felt a shoving on my left shoulder. "What are you doing?" I asked, brusquely. "I was napping."

Glancing up, I saw Shaneika pointing. "LOOK! LOOK!"

I followed her outstretched hand and saw the campground lit up like a sparkler. "Jumping Jehoshaphat! It's the row your RV is in!"

A giant blaze shot up to the sky as people tried to put the fire out with car extinguishers and water. We heard fire trucks in the distance.

"Hurry, Shaneika. It might be yours, and Baby is inside." My insides clutched with fear. We drove down the incline to the park and around to our row parking some distance from the flames.

It *was* Shaneika's RV on fire!

"BABY!" I screamed, jumping out of the van and running toward the RV. "BABY!" I was near hysterics, pushing people out of my way trying to get close to the burning vehicle.

"You can't go in there," a man yelled, grabbing me by my waist and pulling me away from the RV. "Get back, lady, or you'll get burned. Did you say there's a baby inside?"

"My dog! My dog is inside. Did anyone get my dog out?" Tears were streaming down my cheeks as I was near collapse. I just couldn't take any more loss today.

"Is this your dog?" I heard a woman say.

11

I whipped around to see a woman with dark hair clasping Baby by his collar. For a moment, I thought it was Magda Dane holding him, but this woman was taller. Not much, maybe an inch or so.

Baby strained at the woman's hold and broke free, running over to me. I burst into a new crying jag as Baby pressed against my legs looking up with his tail wagging. "Yes. Yes, he's mine. Thank you."

"I was taking a walk and passing by when I heard him barking and saw the smoke. I got him out before the fire broke loose."

"Thank you so much. I am grateful. Very grateful."

"I love dogs, too. Glad I could be of help."

"May I ask your name?"

"I am Margot Dane. My sisters are working on the dig. Perhaps you have met them—Magda and Maja?"

My blood chilled. "Yes, I've met them."

A loud horn blasted. The fire trucks had arrived, and the police instructed everyone to move out of the way. Through the gathering of people, I saw Shaneika speaking with the Fire Marshall. When turning back around, I strained my neck looking for Margot, but she was gone. Margot Dane had disappeared.

"Come on, Baby. Let's get out of this mess." Baby and I waited in my van with the doors locked. I took pictures of the crowd with my phone, one of the few times I had ever used its camera. I couldn't hear what people were saying, so I got out of the van and sat at a picnic table. Baby and I were near the drama but still out of harm's way when I spied the Dane's gleaming RV standing unattended. Where were the Danes? Looking around, I saw Gavin and Magda watching near the fire truck. Did I dare? Should I dare? Why not!

Baby and I quietly moseyed over to the unoccupied RV. "Stand guard, Baby," I said before knocking on the opened door. Stepping up into the RV, I poked my head inside. "Hello? Anyone here? Hello!"

No answer. That was good because I had to lift my tongue off the floor after seeing the opulence of the RV. The entire inside was pallid with white leather couches and banquette with white high gloss accents and kitchen cabinets with porcelain tile floor through-out. Over the farmer's sink was a silver metallic and glass backsplash with silver metallic accents throughout the entire RV. It had a wide screen TV and surround sound system in the living area with a half bath. The master bedroom hosted a king size bed with yet another TV, cedar closet, and a full bathroom with multiple shower heads and built-in seat. It was a beautiful RV and I loved it, but it didn't stop me from snooping in the built-in cedar drawers. Drats—nothing.

I've got to admit I'm a smart cookie. This luxury RV was built for rich people, and rich people need to hide valuables and guns. So where was the hidden safe? There were no pictures on the walls and no mismatched planks on the floor, so the safe wasn't there. The bed was the obvious answer. It was built on a platform high off the floor with lots of cubic footage underneath to hide stuff. I felt along the base and found a small button on the right side. I shut my eyes and pressed it, hoping an alarm would not go off. A drawer slid open with a metal top requiring a push button key combination accompanied by a fingerprint touchpad. Boy, was this baby high tech. I certainly wouldn't get into the safe without the combination and the correct index finger print.

"WHAT ARE YOU DOING?"

I looked up to see Gavin McCloud flash angry eyes at me as a Dane twin stepped beside him. "Yes, what are you doing, Josiah?"

I surreptitiously pushed the safe drawer closed with my leg as I got up off the bed. "I'm sorry, but I had to sit down for a moment."

"Why are you here?" Magda questioned as she moved inside the bedroom, glancing about. Gavin followed suit.

"Sorry, but which twin are you?" I just wanted to mess with the twin a little bit.

"I'm Magda, of course. Now explain yourself."

I didn't believe one moment that I was speaking to Magda. I believed I was speaking to Maja, but if the woman wanted to play this game, I would join along. There was a chance I was wrong.

My heart started to race as I noticed my exit route blocked. "Margot saved my dog, Baby, from the fire and I wanted to thank her properly." I yelled, "BABY! COME!"

"She's staying at the hotel. This is not Margot's trailer," the Dane twin said.

Thank goodness Baby came lumbering past Gavin and Magda as they jumped out of his way. They looked askance at the drool hanging from his mouth and did not approach me any further. He pressed up against me and circled around to face the couple. Baby didn't like the tension in the room and whined, looking at me for solace with his one good eye. That's the English Mastiff way.

"I'm very sorry. I saw the door was open, and I thought she was here. I called and called and when no one answered, I thought the worst with the door being unlocked, so I checked."

"Everyone is fine. Please leave. You're invading our privacy," Gavin declared.

"So sorry," I apologized again. Rising, I wobbled a bit and fell back on the bed. As the Dane twin rushed toward me, Baby growled and bared his teeth, which proved to me this woman wasn't the real Magda. It was Maja impersonating her sister, but for what reason?

"Goodness," the twin said, jumping back. "I'm just trying to help."

I petted Baby on the head. "He won't hurt you as long as I don't give the command to attack."

Now you know I'm lying and I know I'm lying, but Magda/Maja didn't know I was lying. Since I was lying, might as well take it a step further. "When Margot handed Baby over, I asked her how the family reacted when you told them the family business was being sold."

The Dane woman looked stunned.

"What's being sold? What's this old hag talking about?" Gavin asked.

"Shut up." She spat at Gavin while giving me the evil eye.

I stood up again and leaned on Baby's head for support. "If you see Margot, tell her I was looking for her and good luck with the sale."

Gavin started to say something, but was hushed.

"We'll see ourselves out," I said, motioning for Baby to follow.

The pair backed up against the wall, giving Baby a wide berth. There was room for us both to pass, and I couldn't wait to get out of the RV. I made it out of the luxurious motor home without being hit on the head and went in search of Shaneika. I found her in her rented RV, cleaning up a sooty, soaked mess.

"What's the damage?" I asked.

"Actually, not much. It's scorched here and there. Mostly smoke and water damage, but we can still sleep here tonight if we air it out for the next hour or two. I wish Baby could tell us what happened."

"What was the cause?"

"The chief thinks a lit cigarette was thrown into the wastebasket in the bathroom."

"Did you tell him that neither of us smokes?"

"Yep, and I put a call into Sergeant Trimble. We'll see what she has to say tomorrow."

"You're not quitting?"

Shaneika gave me the evil eye. "What makes you think I'd give up on finding the murderer of my cousin? This conflagration means we are making someone nervous."

"Distant cousin."

"What?"

"Distant cousin."

"Doesn't matter. We were related by blood, history, and culture. Did you know Heather's white great-grandmother hired my black great-grandmother as a cook?"

"Lots of white families hired their black relatives.

Doesn't give them a pass, especially the Warfields who were part of the "Glorious Lost Cause" fairy tale after the Civil War."

"Some Warfields fought for the Union, just like the Todd family did. Remember, it was a war where brother fought against brother," Shaneika countered.

"I'm listening."

"Heather's great-grandmother didn't have to hire my great-grandmother, who had gone to her asking for help because my family was starving during the Depression. Not only did Heather's great-grandmother pay my grandmother a wage, but let her take home all the leftovers, and we are not talking about field-hand leftovers, but white tablecloth, Sunday dinner, pork roast with all the fixings. My black family ate better than some white folks during the Depression."

"What happened to Shaneika the Rebel? Sounds like you are making excuses for white families who made policies that kept black people disadvantaged and poor."

"With history, you have to include the human element into the story. History can't be just about dates, facts, and battles. It has to be about people's motivations and intentions as well—and acts of kindness that extend across social and economic classes. The money my great-grandmother made from being the Warfield's cook allowed my grandmother to train as a nurse. The money she saved allowed my mother to train in the hospitality field. The money my mother made from managing boutique hotels in the Carribean allowed me to go to law school. That branch of the Warfield family was one of my first clients. I was the family lawyer for Heather's mother and then Heather. I've handled all property transfers, Last Will and Testaments, and other legal issues for the family since I opened my practice. Their business kept me afloat in the beginning until I built up my client base."

"Ironic, isn't it?"

"I'm not going to blame my white ancestors for past sins. The past is the past. I can't change it. We need to keep moving forward as one people." Shaneika petted Baby's head. "Josiah, I've got a deep anger inside. It's like a twisted ball wrapped around another twisted ball of anger, and I've got to push it down every day or I can't function. When I think of how my black ancestors suffered, it's like I can't breathe. The only thing I can do is go forward and fight for justice for all people. Fight the system. Fight inequality. Just fight, fight, and fight. That's all I know to do."

"You know my theory on humanity. We are all scumbags."

Shaneika plopped down beside me on the couch. "You are the most cynical person I've ever met. Don't you believe there are good people in the world?"

"I believe that humans are capable of acting on their worst instincts given the right motivation and opportunity."

"Naw, there are people who are inherently good."

"Shaneika Mary Todd, a believer in humanity. Who would have *thunk* it?"

Shaneika gave me a cheeky grin. "What's the game plan tomorrow? We have just one more day before everyone scatters."

"I've already put a plan into motion."

"What's that?"

"Creating dissension among the Dane family. I was snooping in the Dane's RV when Gavin and Magda caught me. The only problem was that it wasn't Gavin and Magda. It was Gavin and Maja posing as Magda."

"Where was Magda?"

"That's the sixty-four dollar question. Where is Magda?"

"What made you think Maja was impersonating Magda?"

"Only Magda and Gavin were staying in that RV, and the most important fact is that Baby scared this woman. Remember Magda coming to our campfire? She was enthusiastic about meeting Baby and loved on him. Baby responded in kind, but he didn't like the woman we encountered in the Dane's RV, and she was obviously afraid of him."

"Afraid of Baby. The only thing anyone should be afraid of with that dog is the goop he leaves on one's clothes."

"He growled at her and bared his fangs."

Shaneika glanced at Baby with renewed respect. "Way to go, Baby."

Baby raised his head from the floor at the sound of his name, his tail thumping on the floor.

"I also brought up the selling of the business, and Gavin appeared not to know what I was talking about. I don't think Magda got a chance to discuss the sale as she was taken out of the picture."

"You think she's dead?"

"I don't know, but let's recount what Heather said to me. She believed Gavin and Maja were planning to eliminate Magda. She told me that Maja said that they had to do it before Monday. Magda told us Monday is when the sale becomes final."

"Did Heather actually say Gavin and Maja used the word 'kill'? Now be very careful here. Nuance is everything."

I had to think back. "She first used the word kill, but I asked Heather to tell me the exact words. Now let me think." I closed my eyes, trying to recall our conversation. "She said she crept closer to the couple and heard Gavin say, 'Let's do this. We can make it look like an accident.' The woman said something like, 'We have to do it soon. Before Monday. I told you she was going ahead with this.'"

"Then the word murder or kill was never used by the couple. What you've told me could mean anything."

"Heather said the man used the word 'accident.'"

"Which could be construed a hundred different ways. Heather interpreted the conversation as a murderous intent. It might not be so."

"Then where is the real Magda Dane McCloud, Shaneika? We have not seen her since we encountered the twins on the beach the morning Heather was found."

"We saw her today with her husband."

"I'm telling you that woman was not Magda Dane. That was Maja impersonating her."

Shaneika insisted, "You're going to have to prove that was not Magda."

"What about fingerprints? Even identical twins have variations in their prints."

"Unless their company has a copy of fingerprints, the twins have never been printed."

"How do you know?"

"Why would they?"

"There is a way. The safe in their RV needs a fingerprint impression to open it. Magda and Gavin are the only ones to have access to the safe."

Shaneika said, "It could need only Gavin's print."

"Why don't we see?"

"This is all conjecture. The sale was a done deal. There was no need to kidnap Magda or worse. It might be that there is one final document Magda has to sign before the deal is finalized. I'm talking hypothetically, but what if Heather overheard Gavin and Magda planning something?"

I said, "Why would they go into the woods at dawn to discuss something in private when they could speak in the comfort of their own RV if that person was the real Magda? Heather brought that point up, and I think Heather got it right. It was Maja and Gavin she saw."

"I'm playing the devil's advocate here. What if the man she saw with one of the Danes wasn't Gavin, but Ellison? Gavin and Ellison are both tall and dark-headed. It was at the break of day, and Heather was nearsighted."

"We are going in circles. If it was Ellison, Heather would recognize the man she loved even in bad light. Ellison and Maja. I don't see it. It makes more sense for Gavin and Maja to be plotting something. In the end, we've got all these suspects, but no concrete motives or proof of anything."

Leaning over, Shaneika grabbed a small bag off the kitchen counter and popped a potato chip in her mouth. "No, we don't. We have theories, but nothing to back any of them up. Give me one that will hold up in a court of law."

"Becky lied about finding Heather."

"The camp manager could be the one lying. Let's stick with the facts."

I said, "We think somehow Heather was lured outside and murdered between this RV and her car."

"Again, a theory."

"But there is evidence showing that is what happened."

"Depends on how the prosecutor interprets the evidence."

Frustrated, I said, "Shaneika, quit thinking like a lawyer. Think like a cop."

Shaneika popped some more chips into her mouth and fed one to Baby.

"We think Heather would not open the RV door to Gavin or Maja, but she might have to Ellison. There was no sign of forced entry, so she must have trusted the person to let them in. And there was no commotion that woke you up."

"I agree."

"Okay. Heather opens the door, and she leaves voluntarily."

Shaneika nodded her head. "The State Police concurred that there were no signs of a struggle inside the RV or right outside the RV door. The car keys and disturbed ground were found between the RV and her car. The evidence indicates that she was tased from the behind while going to her car. The stun gun marks prove that. Then she was carried to the Kentucky River and thrown in."

"I'm not buying that Heather was dead before she hit the water. I think the final medical report will state that water was in her lungs, but she may have been unconscious when thrown in."

"I hope she was dead before being tossed into the water. Drowning is not a pleasant way to go."

I said, "If I were going to kill Heather, I would have thrown her body into the trunk of her car and dumped the car into the river at a different location. They had the keys. Why drag her all the way to the river here? It was getting light and people were starting to stir. The murderers took an awful risk."

"One is that Heather's death had to look like an accident. Two is that they couldn't find her keys since they were dropped and had to get rid of the body fast."

"The keys wouldn't have been hard to find as Heather must have been holding them as she walked to her car."

"Unless the murderer panicked. After all, people were starting to rise. Time was precious."

Shaneika said, "We know there were two distinct points of trauma from a stun gun on her body which leads the police to believe two people were in on this, but I think a single person could have attacked Heather holding the stun gun and hit her twice."

"We need to find that stun gun."

"It could be at the bottom of the Kentucky River."

"I think it will turn up eventually in order to frame someone."

"Who?"

I said, "Not sure yet, but I believe the killer is still here. He will stay until the dig is over because he doesn't want to draw attention to himself by leaving."

"What do you think is going to happen?"

"A lot depends on what Sergeant Trimble is going to do. One thing is for certain. Only one Dane twin will show up at the dig tomorrow."

Shaneika looked at her watch. "Which is coming sooner than you think. Let's get some shut eye. I need to rest."

"I need sleep, too. Give the brain time to relax."

"As if your brain is ever hitting all cylinders."

I made a face. "Who has solved multiple murders before the police did?"

"And they simply adore you for getting in their way."

I made a raspberry.

"There's going to be a gathering at eight to honor Heather. Will you come?"

"Of course. We need to see who shows up."

"See you tomorrow then."

"Goodnight, Shaneika."

"Night, Josiah." Shaneika said before yawning and drifting off to bed.

I jammed my suitcase against the RV door and left a light on in the kitchen warning off any others who might think of harming us. After brushing my teeth, I made for my bunk bed, but the covers were wet and smelled of smoke. I found a clean blanket in a drawer and went up front to the captain chairs. I found the passenger's chair would tilt back, so I gratefully climbed into it wearing my day clothes, and wrapped the blanket around as best I could. There was a curtain for my side window which I closed. This was better than sleeping in my van as the RV was higher and no one could see me.

The fire was a sure sign we had some of the pieces to figure out Heather's murderer. They wanted to scare Shaneika and me off. He, she, or they certainly didn't know whom they were dealing with.

I just hoped we got to the perps before they got to us!

12

The camp manager woke me up by rattling metal garbage containers while inserting clean bags into the cans. He threw the filled bags into a golf cart before moving on to the next can and again making a loud racket in the process.

I sat up, rubbing the crick in my neck. I felt horrible. Sleeping in an RV captain's chair is not ideal even though the chair might look comfy. I was stiff and achy.

Baby got up from the bed I had made for him on the floor spry as ever and ready for a new day. He emphasized his insistence by banging his tail against my chair.

"Okay. Okay. I know you have to tinkle, but so do I. I get first dibs." I hurried to the bathroom, did my business, brushed my hair and teeth, but didn't bother to change even though I smelled like smoke. I needed a shower, clean clothes, and a hot meal. First things first though.

Still half asleep, I let Baby out of the RV and followed. He made a beeline for the camp manager. "Good morning."

"Morning." The manager gave me the once over.

I knew even with my ablutions, I looked like a scarecrow and a ratty one at that.

"You folks stay in the RV last night?"

"We thought we'd better. You know how some people are. Some might be tempted to loot," I said, noticing the man's name tag on his tan park uniform said Nate. He was about my age, gray headed, and slumping about the shoulders from years of hard work.

Nate nodded. "Yeah, I know. Never had so much trouble in this campground until this dig. Wish the park guys had never given those archaeologists permission to excavate."

"Nate, do you know who got my dog out during the fire? I'd like to thank him." I wanted to see if Nate gave me a different answer than Margot's explanation.

"Can't tell you. I was too busy calling the fire department and running to get my fire extinguisher."

"Did you discover the fire?"

"Naw. My shift had ended. I was getting ready to leave for home when someone starting yelling 'fire.'"

"Do you know who that was?"

"Don't know. People started yelling and I got into my golf cart to find the fire. Didn't take me long. Just followed the smell of smoke."

"Was it a man or a woman who first yelled fire?"

"Don't rightly know. Can't remember."

"Was the door to the RV open or closed when you got there?"

Exasperated, Nate said, "Lady, I don't remember."

I let my face drop. I always put on the 'pathetic, old lady look' when men don't cooperate. It makes them feel guilty.

It worked! Nate paused. "The door was closed but unlocked. I went inside with the fire extinguisher and put out the fire."

"You put out the fire! I thought the fire department did."

"Things were still smoldering when they got here, so they finished up. Gave the RV a good dose of water."

"Did you let my dog out?"

"Never saw a dog. I would have seen that monster," Nate said, eyeing Baby who was lifting his leg on a garbage can. From the expression on Nate's face, I would hazard a guess he didn't like my dog.

Nate's answer told me that whoever started the fire had let Baby out first. "When Ms. Todd and I were coming back from dinner, we saw fire flash in the sky almost like a beam."

"That was the back of the RV. The fire crawled up the back wall of the RV, but the firemen got it out."

"Is that normal?"

"You'd have to ask a fire expert, but your RV is an older model. She's still a pretty thing, but constructed in the 1970's. Really considered an antique."

"It's a rental."

"I'm surprised it was legal to rent her out being so old. Maybe the manufacturer wasn't using fireproof materials at the time of construction. I wouldn't know."

"Here, let me help you," I said, gathering some of the filled garbage bags and tossing them into the golf cart. Although the bags were full, they were light.

"Thanks," Nate said gratefully before going on with his work.

I followed. "One last question please, and then I'll quit bugging you."

"Promise?"

"Who first told you about finding Heather Warfield?"

"Kayakers discovered her."

"Were they people you knew?"

The camp manager huffed, "I knew it wasn't going to be the last question."

I gave him my pitiful look again. "Please?"

"There were two who ran into the store. They told me about finding the body and that several others were fishing her body out from the river."

"Do you know who?"

"The kayakers in the store were a young couple. I don't know their names, but they are regulars on the river. I think they live several miles to the west in a log cabin—back to the land wannabees. You know the type—want to farm until they discover farming is a lot of work and then they hightail it back to the city. They are always out early in their kayaks on the weekends. They were shook up for sure and wanted me to notify the park rangers and the police which I did."

"Who pulled Heather's body out of the water?"

"Ellison Brody and Dr. Reese."

"Is that so? About what time?"

"It was early. The sun had crested so I say a little before seven."

"Did you talk to Rebecca that morning?"

"Who?"

"Becky. She's dark-headed, about 35, petite, and one of the archaeologists."

"One of those dark-headed gals with the silver shock at their widow's peak? No, I never saw either one of them that morning."

I gaped at Nate. Until he had said it, I hadn't realized how much Becky resembled the Dane twins. "No, she's one of the archaeologists," I repeated.

"I know who you are talking about. She's in the store all the time buying soda and water. She may have been at the river, but by the time I got there, there were several people trying to help. It's all a blur now. I couldn't tell you who all was there."

"Becky never informed you about Heather?"

"No, it was the kayakers."

"How do you know it was Ellison and Dr. Reese, who pulled Heather out of the river?"

"They told me and others concurred."

"Thank you, Nate. You've been most helpful."

"You bet."

I left Nate to his chores and was on my way back to the RV when Sergeant Trimble pulled in with several other police vehicles. I waved and to my surprise, she beckoned to me. Baby and I went over to where Trimble was waiting. "You expect a gunfight today?" I said, after observing six officers standing behind her.

"There are inconsistencies in people's statements. We came to clear them up."

"There's going to be a little volunteer gathering to honor Heather this morning."

"That's another reason why we are here." Trimble ordered several of the men to obtain the cameras from the trunks of the cars. Giving me her full attention again, Trimble said, "I understand there was trouble last night."

"Yeah. Someone set our RV on fire while Shaneika and I were in Richmond having dinner. Thank God someone saved my dog."

"I've already gotten a report on the fire. Minimal damage to the RV. The Fire Chief said he thought a cigarette in a wastebasket started the fire."

"That's mighty curious since neither Shaneika nor I

smoke, and no one had been in our RV since Heather's death except for you."

"I guess we'll be watching to see who smokes today."

I asked, "You staying the entire day?"

"I think our presence might spook the murderer and cause him to act rashly."

"I'm on board with that. There are two things you might want to check today."

"I'm listening."

"One of the archaeologists named Becky lied to me about finding Heather's body. She told me she reported it to the camp manager, but I just talked with him and he said nada. Never happened."

"How sure was he?"

"He seemed pretty clear about it. Who does your intel say reported Heather's death to the camp manager?"

Refusing to answer, Trimble shifted her feet and leaned against her vehicle. "Okay, that's one."

"I think one of the Dane twins is not going to show up today. I think the missing twin will be Magda Dane."

"That's two."

"Might want to talk with Margot Dane. She said she saved my dog, but she's staying in town, so what was she doing at the campgrounds at ten at night?"

"Perhaps visiting her sisters. That's three. What else you got?"

"Have it your way," I said. "Just trying to help."

"Stay out of it, Mrs. Reynolds. I deal with facts. You keep throwing theories at me. I know which direction I wish to pursue."

"Look for Magda Dane today. She won't be here. Mark my words."

Sergeant Trimble pushed off her vehicle, and went over to the river bank, leaving me standing alone. Baby and I followed her to the small knot of people who had gathered for the memorial. Shaneika gave a wonderful tribute about her cousin telling amusing stories of them playing as children, double-dating as teenagers, and how they grew apart as adults only to come together again through the love of history. Other people took turns relating how their lives intersected with Heather's.

Baby and I stood on the periphery of the group scanning the crowd, as did Sergeant Trimble. Dr. Reese sat on a boulder while her husband Ellison, remained on the opposite side of the group. I saw a divorce in their future, but I respected their lack of drama on the dig. If Shaneika hadn't told me about Heather's affair with Ellison I never would have known about the archaeologists' marriage.

I heard a door slam and turned to see Gavin and a Dane twin emerge from the RV and stroll over to our group. *Was it Magda or Maja*, I wondered. I felt Baby tense up and watch them, which only reinforced my theory that Magda was being impersonated by her sister Maja.

I saw Trimble notice them and quickly spin to scan the crowd. I knew she was searching for the other twin sister. So, she did give my theory credence! Slowly, Trimble walked the outskirts of the gathering, while her minions took pictures of the crowd and license plate numbers on cars. Suddenly, Trimble turned on her heels and went over to the McCloud couple, pulling them away from the crowd.

I watched intently as a discussion ensued with Gavin wildly gesturing and Magda storming back to their RV with Trimble following. I decided to follow them. After all, Trimble might need my help. Wink. Wink.

I tiptoed up to within a few feet of the RV where I could hear what sounded like a heated conversation. Darn it! I couldn't make out all the words.

Several minutes later, Trimble came out of the RV looking troubled. She popped a stick of gum into her mouth and watched the crowd disperse, many of them heading over to the dig for the last time.

"Well?"

Startled, Trimble jerked a bit. "Geez, don't sneak up on me like that."

"What cockamamie story did she give you about her twin not going to Heather's memorial service?"

"You're not at the memorial service."

"I was."

"Magda told me Maja went back to Baltimore on an early morning flight."

"I noticed Margot's not here this morning either."

"Meaning what?"

"Margot looks very similar to her twin sisters."

"The woman in this RV showed me a photo ID that had the name Magda Dane McCloud on it. She had a purse filled with Magda's personal effects."

"You gonna check the airport to verify if Maja boarded the flight?"

"Damn right, I am. The woman I just talked with was not the same woman I interviewed days ago. Those sisters look identical, but their mannerisms are different as well as tone of voice. Being a cop, one is trained to notice these things."

"I told you so."

"It's unseemly to crow. Anyone ever tell you that?"

"Constantly. What now?"

"I'm sending an officer to the airport. I should get a report before noon."

As we strode over to the dig, I said, "You know the Dane's RV has a large storage compartment in the back. A perfect place to hide a body."

"Two steps ahead of you, Mrs. Reynolds. Already thought of that, but I have no legal reason to get a warrant. I'll have to wait until my officer reports back to me. Once he confirms no Dane got on the plane, I can get one. Until then I have to wait."

Hearing a commotion, I looked over and saw troopers pull out the garbage bags from the dumpster that Nate had collected that morning. They opened them up onto tarps spread out on the parking lot. I watched while they went through them one and by one.

Obviously distressed, Nate stood by, warning them not to spread garbage into the campgrounds. Seeing that the troopers were not paying any attention to him, Nate returned to the camp store, his face lined with apprehension.

The small group gathered to honor Heather lifted their voice in song—Amazing Grace. Since no one knew the second verse, the singing was short lived. After the singing trailed off, people drifted over to the dig site and began removing the tarps while a few stayed behind and consoled Shaneika.

Ellison handed out tools, clipboards, and collection bags while the designated photographer began taking shots of the final day of the excavation. I took a seat at a picnic table where I could see all the action—the troopers going through the trash, the volunteers working the excavation, and most of the vehicles in the last row next to the river.

"Are you working today?"

I looked up to see Shaneika looming over me. "You're blocking my sun. It's still chilly."

"You've got a jacket on." She glanced at the cloudless sky. "It should be warm this afternoon."

"You really want to discuss the weather?"

Shaneika parked herself on the bench beside me. "I keep thinking what would have happened if I had gotten up early instead of sleeping in."

"You can't go there. Heather had the option of waking you up. She had the option of not opening the RV door. I had the option of taking her with me. There were miscalculations everywhere. The only person to blame is the one who snuffed out Heather's life."

"Do you believe we all have an expiration date and when our time is up, it's up?"

"One of the biggest questions we humans ask ourselves. I don't know, Shaneika, but I don't think Heather had to die. It was the culmination of space and time and evil intent."

"The wrong place at the wrong time."

I replied, "That about sums it up."

"You don't believe in the grand plan?"

"I believe in wickedness."

My answer hung in the air as we sat in silence, each in our own thoughts. Shaneika is not the huggy type and neither am I, but I wondered if Shaneika needed comforting. This is something I'm not good at. If I do, I usually blurt out the wrong thing, so I've learned to keep my mouth shut in most situations regarding grief. I don't need to exhibit my cynicism to the world, especially when someone is suffering. I believe in deeds, not words, so you won't hear me wax ceremoniously at a funeral or even at a happy occasion like a wedding. I'm not that sort of camper. I show my affection through cooking, gifting, and doing favors for friends.

I glanced at Shaneika and saw her eyes glistening with tears. I realized I should do something. She was my friend and she was hurting. I reached over and squeezed her hand. "I'm not going to say it will be okay because it won't. I will say you will get through this. Maybe not stronger or better as the 'Pollyannas' of this world would say, wanting to shove that silly blindly optimistic outlook down your throat when things go wrong. I'm not going to say this was God's will, because I don't believe that either, but you will survive, and I will be beside you."

Shaneika didn't look at me, but squeezed my hand in return.

We continued in silence until I asked, "Her parents coming?" I had enough of this sentimentality. I needed to cut through the gloom.

"They will fly up as soon as the body is released. They're having a very private funeral with just immediate relatives from this area. I think they want Heather cremated, so they can take her with them when they return to Florida."

I didn't have time to respond as we noticed Trimble hurrying into the woods on the west side of the grounds. "Something's afoot," I said, quoting my favorite detective—Sherlock Holmes.

Shaneika pulled me to my feet, and we scurried over to where we could hear the troopers.

Trimble glanced up from her little circle of officers and spotted us.

To our surprise, she gestured to us.

We shambled down a small knoll and stood before her little knot of crime solvers.

"Have you found something?" Shaneika asked, eager for some good news, even a kernel.

Trimble thrust an evidence bag at her. "Do you recognize this phone?"

Shaneika took the bag and studied it. "This is Heather's. See the UK basketball decal on the back." She handed the bag back to Trimble.

Trimble offered the bag to me.

I held up my hand, waving the bag off. "I never looked at Heather's phone. I couldn't tell you if it was hers or not."

Shaneika asked, "Where did you find it?"

"One of the troopers found it stuck down a rabbit hole. That's not all." She turned to one of her assistants. "Show them."

A female trooper held up a bag—one with a stun gun.

"You found it!" Shaneika exclaimed.

"I doubt it will be useful as I'm sure there won't be

any identifiable prints," Trimble said, "but you never know."

"Where did you find it?" I asked.

"Under a rock buried at the foot of a tree. We found it only because the ground looked disturbed."

Waving away a bug from my face, I asked, "What happens now?"

"I will get a warrant to search every vehicle and camper that was here on the day of Miss Warfield's death."

Shaneika asked, "What's the news at the Baltimore airport? Was it Magda who got off that plane?"

"No," Trimble simply said.

"Who was it?" I asked, my heart beating faster as the adrenaline shot into my veins. We were getting close on the hunt.

"The Baltimore police have identified the woman using Magda's ticket was her sister, Margot Dane. She's been detained for questioning, but Magda Dane is not officially missing. No one has filed a missing persons report."

Shaneika said, "They can hold her on falsely using Magda's ID to get on a plane. Whose did she use?"

"Magda Dane's passport." Trimble held up her hand to ward off our protests. "I know what you are going to say. How did Margot get Magda's passport and why did she use it?"

"If the woman with Gavin is really Magda Dane,

where is Maja Dane? The other twin has not shown up today," I added. "One of the twins is missing." I just had to get the last word in.

"I am waiting for the warrants and to hear from the Baltimore police report, but Gavin and Magda Dane, or whichever twin she is, will be pulled in today for questioning."

"The sooner, the better," Shaneika huffed.

Trimble replied, "The day is still young, and we have a lot of work to do before that happens. I would appreciate it if you two would go about your business and leave this investigation to the professionals. You two are acting like stalkers."

We had to admit Trimble was correct. Shaneika and I knew we were becoming a hindrance to the police now, so we would bide our time until we could step in again. We made sure Trimble had our phone numbers before we drifted off.

I said, "One more thing, Sergeant Trimble. The Dane's RV has a secret safe under the master bed. It requires a fingerprint impression besides a numerical code. If I were you, I'd be looking for a detached finger, too."

Trimble's eyes widened. "Thanks for the tip. I'll keep that in mind."

Shaneika went back to the dig, as I headed over to the replica of Fort Boonesborough to kill some time.

Time wasn't the only thing that was to be killed.

13

The life-sized replica of Fort Boonesborough was a short distance from our dig, but still too far for me to walk with my bad leg, so I rented a golf cart from the camp store since our vehicles weren't allowed off the grounds until they had all been searched. I left the keys in my van, pretty sure no one would steal it with all the cops around.

Baby and I first putt-putted over to the pool area and watched the workers furiously cleaning and painting the facility getting ready for the upcoming swim season. The pool was in a pretty area overlooking the Kentucky River and the Palisades. It was a nice pool, but should have been three times the size for the number of people it served.

I think all city and state pools should have a section of the pool that is off limits to children at all times. Children scream, splash, push, and are in general unpleasant in and around water. They also pee in the water. Come on, we all know it.

It seems to me that the people, who pay for these pools, i.e. adults, never get to enjoy them in peace, but then you know my opinion of children in general—best seen, not heard. Of course, there are parents who gladly drop their kids off for an afternoon's swim so they can have an hour of calm sipping their Bloody Marys and reading a good mystery. That's what I would do if I didn't have a pool of my own. After watching the workmen for a while, I scooted over to the fort, parking my cart near the entrance.

After paying for a ticket and a pamphlet, I entered the fort. Since Baby stayed glued by my side, no one said he couldn't enter, so we wandered about. There were several sheep happily grazing in a grass enclosure surrounded by log walls, log houses, and two-story blockhouses with slits on the back walls for musket barrels to slide through to shoot at enemies of which there were aplenty at the time the fort was built. After all, the European settlers were breaking the treaty and trespassing on Native American land.

I sat on a bench reading my pamphlet and observing the fort. Near the back, a blacksmith banged away at his outdoor forge while a reenactment actress, dressed in eighteenth-century garb, boiled water in a huge kettle demonstrating how the frontiersmen washed their clothes. I'm being facetious here when I say "frontiersmen." We know who carried the wood and hauled the water to boil and sanitize the wash—

wives, children, African slaves, and European "indentured servants," which is a polite term for temporary slaves. They served a seven or a fourteen year contract in exchange for passage to the New World, but people could be forced to work as such for a myriad of reasons.

Lexington's most famous indentured servant was a white man named William "King" Solomon, who was a chronic alcoholic. After being arrested once too often for public drunkenness in 1833, Solomon was sold as an indentured servant for nine months to work off his sentence and pay his court fees. Solomon was purchased for pennies by Aunt Charlotte, a free black woman. Before Solomon could work off his debt, cholera broke out. Aunt Charlotte fled Lexington, but Solomon stayed behind to bury the dead. The town drunk is now remembered as a hero. Funny how things turn out.

Getting back to the problem of cleanliness, hunters wore buckskins which were never washed except with clay rubbed into the outfit once in a great moon, and the "long hunters" did not wear undergarments. You can imagine how the backside of their buckskins looked. They would maybe change their buckskins once a year or when they wore out. Other pioneers wore linsey-woolsey, a fabric woven from wool and flax.

I sat on a bench and imagined what the fort looked

like when the pioneers lived in it. There were no roads or wide trails—just traces that the bison pounded into the ground with their hooves or Indian trails. Stepping off the traces, one stepped into either a dark forest or clusters of canebrakes which grew up to twenty feet.

The log houses had packed dirt floors and the common area was a sodden mess where straw and cane reeds were strewn about to keep shoes and moccasins from seeping into the mud saturated with animal fecal matter. Imagine the stench from the humans and animals on a hot summer day, and the misery caused by flies and mosquitoes. Probably the only relief they got from the insects was the smoke from their cooking fires. However, washing clothes and themselves to get rid of lice, fleas, and other parasites was secondary to other concerns—like staying alive.

The pioneers couldn't wait until they could strike out on their own and escape the filth of the fort, but that wouldn't happen for some time. In fact, they had to stay tied to the fort because of Native American and British attacks. The most famous of these attacks was the Siege of Boonesborough on September 7-18, 1778. A company of Shawnee, Cherokees, Wyandots, Miamis, Delawares, Mingos, and French-Canadian militiamen from Detroit, now fighting on behalf of the British Crown, attacked the fort. It was a fight to the death as the Native Americans considered the pioneers trespassing on their land, but the entire conflict began earlier with the innocent collection of salt. Yes, salt.

The settlement of Boonesborough could not exist without salt. It was how the pioneers preserved their meat. Salt was also used as a seasoning when cooking their bland diet. Spices, sugar, honey, butter, and fruit jams were in short supply for the limited victuals the pioneers were forced to eat. Salt made eating pioneer food bearable.

In January of 1778, Boone led a party of thirty men to a salt lick on the Licking River near Blue Licks to gather it. Still processing salt in February Boone and his men were captured by the great chief of the Shawnee, Blackfish, and taken to Chillicothe where Boone was separated from his men. The Shawnee wanted to kill the European intruders in retaliation for the death of Shawnee Chief Cornstalk, who was murdered by Virginia militiamen. Boone gave an impassioned speech before the tribal council, thus saving his men. However, Boone was forced to run the gauntlet. Impressed with his courage, Boone was adopted by the Shawnee and given free rein while the rest of his men were carted off to Fort Detroit as prisoners of war. Boone, now called Sheltowee, meaning Big Turtle, even escorted ten of his men as prisoners to Detroit. Returning to Chillicothe with Blackfish, he gave every impression of "going native."

In June, Boone learned Blackfish intended to attack Boonesborough and wipe it out. Stealing a horse,

Boone escaped. When his horse collapsed, Boone ran the rest of the 160 miles to warn Boonesborough of the coming threat. It took him five days to reach Boonesborough. This was without boots, compass, maps, matches, food, or potable water.

In September, Native Americans, numbering 444 alongside 12 white men, lay siege to the fort where only 30 men and 20 boys returned fire. The womenfolk put on male clothing to make the enemy think there were more men inside the fort than there were. After days of trying to burn the fort down, digging tunnels, and staging frontal attacks, the Native Americans drifted back into the forest. Thirty-seven Native Americans were dead in contrast to two dead settlers, including a slave named London who was twenty-four years old and shot in the head.

After the danger was over, Boone traveled to North Carolina to bring his family back since Rebecca Boone, assuming Daniel was dead, had returned home. On the return to Kentucky, Boone brought more settlers with him, including a Captain Abraham Lincoln, grandfather of President Abraham Lincoln. Turning his back on Fort Boonesborough forever, Boone settled with his son, Israel, at Boone's Station.

I put the pamphlet away after reading it and wandered around the fort grounds with Baby trailing behind. I watched a woman carding wool in one log house and a woodworker making wooden nails in another. I wondered how it was for men and women to work and live in such close proximity with no privacy and very few comforts of home while risking their lives for the grand prize of all—land. It has long been a legend that the first thing these people did was to grow corn, but not always for the dinner table. Much of the corn went to making whiskey. I certainly understood why. If I had to live in such a place for months or even years, I would be drinking, too.

Baby was bored. Not even the sheep currently grazing in the common area interested him, so he lay in the shade of a tree.

"You stay," I said. "I don't want to go chasing after you."

Baby sneezed before flopping on his side to enjoy a quick snooze. Satisfied Baby would not move and no one was going to steal a two hundred twenty pound dog, I wandered into the gift shop.

I meandered about the shop, picking up some books about colonial life, cleaned the store out of quality beeswax candles, and inspected a replica of a Kentucky Long Rifle. Long rifles are not rifles as we know them today, but flintlock guns with spiral grooved barrels holding a single lead ball loaded from the muzzle. Sounds rather primitive, but in the hands of a marksman, they were quite accurate and deadly. It was believed that an experienced marksman or woman could fire three shots per minute. That includes pouring gunpowder down the barrel, shoving a "patched" ball tamped down on top of the powder with a ramrod. After a finer grade of gunpowder was poured into the pan of the gun, the hammer was cocked and the rifle was ready to fire. Even with all those steps, experts were still able to get off three shots per minute while staying cool under pressure when an angry bear or an enemy rushed them. I don't know if I could be so calm following all those steps and then raise the gun, aim, and fire under such strenuous circumstances, but I guess when one's life is in danger, a person can do anything.

I asked the store clerk several questions about the rifle as I thought of buying it for my boyfriend, Hunter, who was working in New York City on a new case. She said the gun was made by a local gunsmith with the same techniques a pioneer would employ to make one in the 1700s. After looking at the price tag, I gingerly put the gun back. It was too rich for my blood.

When placing my loot by the cash register, I spied a case of jewelry. I love jewelry, so I immediately thumbed through picking up a pair of Kentucky agate earrings. "Can you tell me something about these earrings?"

The teenage clerk popped her bubble gum and leaned on her elbows peering into the case. She was wearing an eighteenth-century muslin dress with a contemporary synthetic purple sweater. On her feet were expensive tennis shoes with striped socks. "Those are really nice. We have a local man who makes them. He collects the agate from streams hereabouts."

"I notice these earrings have a red vein in them and the other pairs don't."

"We had three pairs of them with the red made from the same geode. If you look at the price tag, you will see that they are more expensive than the others because red in agate is rare. Jewelry made from agate with red veins is more prized."

"You said you had three pairs of them?"

"Yeah. Some lady bought the other two pairs as gifts for her girlfriends. She took a long time picking them out as she wanted them to be special."

"When was that?"

The clerk looked up at the ceiling contemplating. "I'd say t'was Thursday afternoon right before we closed."

"Did she buy anything else?"

The clerk shook her head. "Not that I recall. She said she wanted to surprise her friends on Sunday with them. I put each pair in a little box and wrapped them up real nice in butcher's paper and twine."

I pulled out my phone and clicked on the photo app. "Do you see anyone in these photos who was the customer?"

The young woman studied the photos from Heather's memorial service and handed back my phone. "I don't see her. Sorry."

I thumbed back to a picture of Heather on the dig and handed the phone back over. "What about this lady?"

The clerk studied the picture on the phone and nodded. "Yeah, that's her."

"You're positive?"

"Of course, I am. Not many people come through here this time of year. I would remember someone buying those earrings. They are expensive. Hey, what's this all about? Is this the lady who drowned? Is that who purchased those earrings?"

I pulled money from my wallet and pushed my earrings, candles, and books into the blue cotton twill bag I was lugging around. "Keep the change, please. You've been most helpful."

"I don't see how, but glad to be of service." The teenager gave me a generous smile.

"May I have my phone back, please?"

"Ah, sure," the clerk said, handing it over.

"One more thing before I leave," I said, thumbing through the pictures again. "Have you ever seen these ladies?"

The young lady pushed back her braided blonde hair and straightened her glasses. "Gee, those ladies look like identical twins. It's like seeing double."

"Have they ever been in here?"

"Not to my knowledge. It's spring break from

school, so I've been working full time in the gift shop since Thursday. I open and close it."

"When you say close it, does that mean you have the key?"

"Yep. I open and lock up." She cracked her gum again, which seemed so out of place as the pioneers didn't chew strawberry gum.

"What about when you are on a break?"

"The lady in the next log house covers for me, but she would tell me if someone came in. Besides, we have cameras." She pointed to the ceiling.

I followed her finger and spied the several surveillance cameras following our every move.

"Do these cameras record?"

"What's the point of having them if they don't record?"

"I quite agree, but you'd be surprised at the number of businesses that don't pay attention to their surveillance cameras."

"We have to keep ours in good condition in case we are sued for something. You wouldn't believe the stunts people pull, and Lord forbid if some kid gets stung by an insect—like we can control nature." The teenager made a derisive sound with her nose.

"I see. How often do you delete the information?"

"We store all info for about one season to the next."

"I'm surprised you are open this weekend."

"We opened this weekend at Dr. Reese's request. There are five staff members who are getting paid to work Thursday through Sunday from 2 pm to 6 pm to give everyone on the dig a chance to visit the fort."

"Most unusual. Who's paying for this? The taxpayer?"

The clerk shrugged. "Dr. Reese, I guess."

"Not the state?"

"No, our pay is covered under the grant."

"Have you gotten paid yet?"

"Dr. Reese gave me a check an hour ago." She pulled it out of her dress pocket and showed me. "See."

I bent over the counter and studied the check. "It's most generous."

"Yeah, extra pay and a bonus. I could sure use it."

"Thank you. You've been very helpful."

"Enjoy those earrings," the teenager called after me emphasizing with one last snap of her gum.

I hurried outside with my purchases to find two of the sheep sniffing Baby, who was deep in sleep. I knew he was dreaming by the kicking of his legs—probably dreaming about chasing sheep. "Baby, come!"

Baby snapped forward, and upon seeing two sheep close to him, jumped to his paws and drew back with a yelp. He seemed confused by the curious ewes still with their winter wool. The abundance of wool enveloping their bodies made the ewes look massive with dark eyes peering out from a dirty white mass of fleece.

"I guess I should be glad the sheep weren't wolves. Come on, Baby. These ewes aren't going to hurt you." I laughed at Baby's startled expression, but I think it hurt his feelings. Baby gave me a wounded look before rushing ahead of me to the parking lot. He wanted no part of those strange creatures, even though they had the wonderful smell of manure clinging to their backsides. Baby liked grass fed manure, especially fresh green manure to roll in on a warm day. That's the best kind apparently. I had to build a fence around my manure compost pile as it became one of Baby's favorite haunts. Manure to Baby was like nectar to honeybees, but not today it seemed. Baby jumped into the cart while I followed, still chuckling.

"Jumping Jehoshaphat!" I exclaimed, looking at my watch. "We've got to get back. It's late."

I had wolves of my own to fend off.

14

When I got back to the camp store, several volunteers were sitting in the porch rocking chairs watching a bulldozer push dirt onto the archaeological site. "Hey guys."

"Where have you been all day?" one woman asked me, obviously put out with me not helping with the dig.

"Sleuthing."

"What?"

"Never mind," I said, watching Sergeant Trimble and another officer talk with Ellison Brody.

The woman turned to her husband. "What did she say?"

"She said to mind your own business," the husband replied, winking at me in solidarity before returning to the consumption of his Moon Pie and RC Cola.

The woman scoffed and turned her chair away from me.

I was baffled as to why the woman took such umbrage with me, but was relieved that I wouldn't have to talk with her further. I had a feeling she found displeasure in most people.

Becky came upon the camp store porch, after knocking mud off her boots on the bottom step. "Hey, Josiah."

"Hey, Becky. What's the latest with the State Police?"

"They've checked everyone's vehicles, the trash, and Lord knows what else. Most people have been cleared to go home."

"Who hasn't?"

"Dr. Reese, Ellison, Shaneika, all of the Danes, you, and me."

"You know what that means?"

"Yeah, we are suspects."

"Did she say we are suspects in that girl's murder?" the bewildered woman asked her exasperated husband.

"Yes," he teased. "We'd better go before the cops put the finger on us."

"Oh, dear," the woman said, thinking her husband was in earnest. "Let's go, Lester. You can finish your Moon Pie in the car."

Lester helped his wife from the rocking chair and she went on ahead. The husband stopped to pet Baby, who was lounging by my rocking chair. "My wife means well," he muttered, giving Baby a small piece of his Moon Pie.

Baby gently accepted the tidbit.

"Nice dog."

"Thank you."

"Goodbye and good luck with the authorities."

I nodded to the gentleman and swiveled to speak with Becky when I noticed she stood frozen, staring at me. "What's wrong, Becky?"

Becky broke from her gaze. "Oh, what? Sorry, I was lost in thought for a second. Excuse me, but I need to get something from the store."

"Sure."

Becky entered the store, allowing the door to slam which reverberated off the Palisades. Sergeant Trimble and her trooper buddy looked over giving an opportunity for Ellison to run for the hills. He ran like Old Scratch himself was after him.

I jumped up from my chair and pointed. "Your man is blowing the joint!"

Trimble's shoulders slumped as she spied Ellison escaping and quickly spoke into her walkie-talkie.

"What's all the commotion?" Becky asked, coming out of the store.

"Looks like Ellison is being arrested for something," I said, watching other troopers surround Ellison. When he resisted, the troopers threw him to the ground.

Becky brought her fingers to her mouth in shock. "For Heather's murder? He didn't kill her."

"Yeah, I know."

"What's that?"

"I know Ellison didn't kill Heather."

"How do you know that?"

"See these earrings," I said, pointing to the agate earrings I was now wearing. "Heather originally purchased two sets of earrings for Shaneika and myself. When the murderer killed her, he took the earrings as a memento and hid them, but not well enough. I found them."

Becky glanced at the bulldozer pushing dirt back onto the site. "Was it Gavin then?"

"What makes you think a man killed Heather?"

"You used the pronoun *he*."

I cautioned, "Could have been a *they* or a *she*."

"I wouldn't be throwing around accusations like that, if I were you. This is a deadly business."

"Exactly."

"How do you know Heather purchased those earrings?"

"Her purchase was recorded on the Fort Boonesborough gift shop security cameras. Heather only purchased the earrings with red in the agate. The clerk will testify to that."

Becky sat in a rocking chair across the camp store entrance from me and opened her bag of potato chips and a can of soda pop. She ate nervously watching Ellison handcuffed and led away as Dr. Reese rushed to his defense. Two troopers put him in a car and drove away.

Dr. Reese and Trimble shared heated words until Trimble broke and strode over to the camp store.

"Seems like Dr. Reese still has the torch for Ellison. Otherwise, she wouldn't have tried to interfere with his arrest."

"Yeah, it seems like it," Becky said absently-mindedly.

"I wonder if Ellison's arrest will have a negative effect on Dr. Reese's career."

"Maybe Ellison is just a 'person of interest?'"

I replied, "I don't think so. They don't cuff a 'person of interest.'"

"He resisted."

"Yeah, that was stupid of Ellison. Very stupid. Makes him look guilty."

Stomping onto the store porch, Trimble said, "Glad to find you both. Saves me some time. I need you both to go the State Police Station 7 right now."

"What for?" Becky asked.

"We're putting this murder to bed tonight, but I need formal statements from everyone."

Becky said, "Haven't you dogged us enough? You know Ellison didn't kill Heather."

"I've got Heather Warfield's murder to wrap up and a possible kidnapping/murder of Magda Dane on my hands. I'm getting to the bottom of it tonight. Be at the station in twenty minutes or I'll have you arrested. Either way, I'm going to interrogate each of my suspects tonight."

"I'm free," I said. "I'd like to talk to you about some earrings and show you some video footage—."

Trimble spoke hurriedly, breaking me off in mid-sentence. "Bring Shaneika Todd with you. Where is she, by the way?"

"Cleaning her RV. I'll fetch her and we'll be there, Trimble."

"Sergeant Trimble to you."

"Yes, ma'am." There is a certain tone women use when they have been trifled with enough. To keep poking them is to invite being poked back with a fury. Trimble was using that tone now.

I turned to Becky. "You want to ride with us?"

"No, thank you. I have my own car."

"See you at the station," I said to both women, as I rose and motioned to Baby. I felt pretty good as I was close to identifying the murderer.

Just a few more lies to set the trap.

15

"Where's your sister?" asked Sergeant Trimble, looking very unhappy.

"I assumed she would be here as ordered," Magda said, clutching on to Gavin's arm.

"Did both of your sisters leave town?" Trimble asked, hoping for a reply in which she could trap the woman sitting before her.

"I don't know."

Trimble slid her phone to Magda across the conference table. "Call one of them."

Everyone sitting around the conference table watched the phone glide across the polished surface of the table top.

Magda picked up the phone and dialed. "No answer." She looked at the phone confused.

"No one is answering because we picked up your sister, Margot, at the airport as she disembarked the plane. She had two phones. One is registered in her name and the other in Magda's name, but we'll get back to Margot later."

"I have my phone," Magda said, holding it up.

"Would you like to tell me what your name is again?"

"I am Magda Dane McCloud."

Trimble said, "We shall see."

"I don't have to be here. I can lawyer up," Magda said.

"Then I would have to issue a statement to the press that we believe one of the Dane sisters is missing. Wouldn't that make an awful lot of bad news on the street for your company? I don't think the Navy would like that. Oh, wait. The Dane Company has been sold, but full payment is to be remitted in thirty-two equal payments. If the value of Dane Enterprises falls, the purchasing company has time to withdraw their offer."

"What's she talking about?" Gavin asked, withdrawing his arm from around Magda. "What deal? Who has bought the Dane Company? What's she talking about?"

"Shush," Magda said.

"We called the company's lawyer after we arrested Margot on suspicion of kidnapping. She sang like a bird."

"I am telling you that I am Magda Dane. I don't know where my sister is."

"And yet you have your sister, Margot Dane, confessing to impersonating you with your passport. You know that is a felony since 9/11."

"I don't know anything about it."

Trimble pulled out her phone and showed a picture of a scarf. "We retrieved this from your RV. Would you say this is Magda Dane's scarf?"

Magda nodded at the checkered blue and white wool neck scarf.

"Mr. McCloud, is this your wife's scarf?"

Gavin glanced at the woman sitting beside him. When she did not respond to his nudge, he mumbled, "Yes."

"You are both saying this is Magda Dane's scarf?"

Gavin huffed, "We said so, didn't we?"

Trimble gave a ghost of a smile and mumbled into her shoulder microphone. A trooper, wearing gloves, took the scarf and left the conference room.

All of us sat quietly in contemplation waiting for Trimble to ask the next question. Gavin was fidgety and broke out into a sweat while I checked the messages on my phone. Becky and Shaneika gazed about the room and then at Trimble, wondering why they were waiting in silence. Magda sat with her eyes closed while Dr. Reese seethed in silence.

A trooper brought in Ellison and told him to sit down. Dr. Reese jumped to her feet, but Trimble cautioned her, "Don't leave your seat. Stay where you are."

"This is most unconventional," Reese complained, trying to catch Ellison's eye as he continued to look away from her.

"Not to say unconstitutional," Gavin huffed. "I know our rights."

"You can leave and lawyer up anytime," Trimble said. "But if you do, I'll release to the papers that you are a suspect in a murder case. All I'm asking is an hour of your time. I don't think that is too much to ask."

No one spoke.

Trimble looked about the room. "Good, then we will proceed." She spoke into her shoulder mic again. A minute later the hallway door opened and a commotion commenced accompanied by the sound of nails scraping on the hallway tile floor and loud baying. A Bloodhound rushed into the room and its trainer released his leash. The Bloodhound kept his nose close to the tile flooring and carefully sniffed each person until it circled back to his owner whereupon he sat and received a treat.

"This is Hazel Mott and this is her dog, Sam. Sam is a certified trained Bloodhound. He is used for tracking people. Now, we have in our possession the scarf I showed you. We let Sam smell the scarf before he was brought into the hallway. Miss Mott, what is your assessment of Sam's behavior?" Trimble asked, her eyes glittering for she knew she was exposing an imposter.

Miss Mott leashed Sam again. "The owner of the scarf is not here."

"I am here," insisted Magda Dane.

Miss Mott said, "If that scarf belonged to Magda Dane, then you are not she. I would bet my professional reputation on it as well as Sam's. Magda Dane is not in this room."

Trimble pulled a cheerful red and orange geometric scarf from a plastic evidence bag. "This scarf was lifted from Maja's room from the B&B this afternoon. Will you please let Sam do his thing?" Trimble said to Mott handing her the evidence bag.

Mott opened the bag and let her dog sniff deeply. "Search."

Sam immediately caught the scent and bounded over to the Dane twin and sat before her baying.

The woman pushed the dog away. "Get this animal away from me."

Gavin argued, "This is ridiculous. Magda and Maja are identical twins. They would smell similar."

Hazel Mott replied, "Not necessarily. This dog has 230 million scent receptors in his nose. He would be able to tell the two sisters apart. Even identical twins have dissimilar scents."

Hazel Mott retrieved her dog, gave him a treat before leashing him.

"Thank you, Miss Mott. That will be all."

Hazel Mott ordered her dog to heel before saying hello to me. "Howdy, Josiah."

"Good to see you again, Hazel. Keeping busy?"

"Yep. See that you're involved in another murder case."

"Seems that way. Glad you could help out."

"I'm just a phone call away. Let's do lunch soon."

"Love to."

Mott was shown out by one of the troopers guarding the door.

"That is not my scarf," the Dane woman insisted.

I swiveled around with my phone, showing my videos. "Actually, it is. If you remember, both you and Magda wore these scarves when you approached Shaneika and me at the beach. I took this video of you both wearing the scarves and introducing yourselves. You each identify yourselves wearing the scarves. My boyfriend taught me how to do this. Otherwise, I'm just thumbs. Give me a minute." I fiddled with the phone and held it up when I swiped to the right video. "See?"

"Let me see that," Sergeant Trimble said, taking my phone and playing back the video. After seeing the video, Trimble placed my phone into an evidence bag. "Sorry, Mrs. Reynolds, but this is evidence now. I have to confiscate it."

"Doesn't matter. I hate those phones anyway. Give me a landline anyway." I turned to the Dane twin. "You are Maja Dane impersonating your sister, Magda."

"I swear this is my wife, Magda."

"Be quiet, Gavin. We want a lawyer."

Ignoring the Dane woman, Trimble said, "We have

another way to check. Boys, bring in the safe."

"What have you done?" Gavin asked.

Trimble said, "We took the liberty of extracting the safe in the Dane RV. We also called the company that made the safe which is the Dane Corporation. I was told by Magda's secretary that the safe required Magda's index finger print when she gave me the combination. So, let's see if she was right."

One of the troopers put the safe near Gavin. Trimble strode over and after looking at a handwritten piece of paper, punched in the code. "Mr. McCloud, would you press your index finger against the touch pad."

Gavin pressed his finger down, but the safe didn't pop open.

Addressing the Dane woman, Trimble asked, "Ma'am, would you care to press your index finger on the touch pad?"

"This is silly. I have nothing to prove and you can't make me."

Trimble grabbed the woman's hand and pressed her index finger on the pad.

The safe did not open.

Everyone stared at the woman pretending to be her sister.

Gavin pushed her away. "I'm not going to jail for you. You said this plan was foolproof."

"Shut up, you idiot. A good lawyer can make mincemeat of this."

"Where is your sister, Maja? Where is your wife, Gavin?" Trimble asked. "Right now, the charges will be suspicion of kidnapping and possibly murder."

"I want to make a deal," Gavin pleaded.

"I'm warning you. Shut up!" Maja hissed.

"Let me call my lawyer, and I'll talk if I'm free of prosecution. I'll sing like a bird. It was all Maja. Not me. I did what I was told."

Maja threw herself at Gavin and attacked him, digging her fingernails into his face before anyone could intervene.

Gavin cried out, "This hellion has wounded me! I can't see out of my eyes! She has ruined my eye!" Blood ran so fiercely down his face, it made me queasy.

Trimble put Maja in handcuffs and handed her over to another officer. "Lock her up."

Shaneika helped another officer put Gavin into an office chair with rollers so he could be scooted out of the room and down the linoleum tiled hallway so they could get him into a car and to a hospital.

During the scuffle, I had retreated into a corner alongside Ellison and Becky. Dr. Reese had remained composed in her seat watching with scientific detachment. Shaneika hadn't moved either.

After both Maja and Gavin had been removed, I sat down next to Shaneika.

She whispered to me, "This kerfuffle is a mess. Trimble has broken every protocol in the book. I see multiple reasons for a lawsuit."

I didn't reply as I was too busy watching everyone else. There were just the five of us now in the conference room. As Ellison sat next to Dr. Reese, he reached for her hand and squeezed it. Sitting across from them were myself, Shaneika, Becky, who seemed quite shaken.

Nonplussed, Trimble handed the safe and the scarves over to the evidence officer.

"If all you're after is the Dane woman, why are we here?" Dr. Reese complained.

"None of the rest of us had anything to do with that."

"We shall see. Don't forget we still have Heather's death on our hands."

A trooper brought in a note and handed it to Trimble. After reading it, she sat back in her chair. "Well, if that don't beat all."

"What shall we do?" asked the officer.

"Put her in an interrogation room. I have a lot of questions." As the officer was on the way out, Trimble called after him, "See if she wants coffee or a soda pop. Get her anything she wants."

Shaneika and I exchanged glances. Something important just happened and I wondered if it had anything to do with Heather.

Trimble stood. "Ladies and Gent, I will have to leave you for a moment.

We just got an important break in the case. I ask for your patience."

Dr. Reese let out a disgusted sigh and looked away in anger.

Ellison said, "Darling, let's stay until this is cleared up. We can't have our reputations stained with suspicion of murder hanging over our heads."

Dr. Reese threw Ellison's hand away. "As if I really mattered to you. Don't talk to me anymore."

Trimble motioned to Shaneika and me. "Will you please follow me?"

Looking somewhat bewildered but curious, Shaneika rose to follow Trimble.

"You, too, Mrs. Reynolds," Trimble said before stepping out of the room.

I locked eyes with Shaneika, who responded by shrugging her shoulders. I hauled my fanny out of the comfy conference chair and followed begrudgingly. I was very close to pulling the plug on Trimble's shenanigans as she legally couldn't hold me. Worn out and needing a new pain patch, I lumbered after Shaneika, who walked briskly down the hallway.

Shaneika was ushered through a door and asked to stay until Trimble came for her.

I followed suit and was given the same instruction.

We were in a room located next to the interrogation room with a two-way mirror.

And whom should we see sitting in the next room

wearing a white wool pantsuit with a white cashmere cape with her black hair pulled back tightly into a bun was none other than Magda Dane!

16

Trimble and another trooper walked in to our room and closed the door. "What do you think?"

"I think you're going to need a good defense lawyer," Shaneika said. "You've falsely arrested two people on suspicion of kidnapping and murder and here sits the supposed victim dressed in Versace."

"They haven't been processed yet, so I'm in the clear."

"Lucky you," Shaneika commented.

"Is that woman Magda Dane?" Trimble asked.

I peered closely through the two-way mirror, almost pressing my nose against the glass. My eyesight was not what it used to be, but then nothing about me was. "The mannerisms are similar, but I can prove conclusively if that is Magda Dane."

Trimble asked, "How?"

"Get Baby. Magda liked Baby and Baby liked her. Maja does not like dogs. Let's see how this woman reacts to Baby."

"What if Baby doesn't go to her?" Shaneika asked.

"Then Sergeant Trimble, you will have to reemploy Hazel Mott and Sam again and pull the safe out of the evidence locker again."

"I have really screwed up," Trimble mumbled.

"I won't disagree with you there," Shaneika said. "We are no closer to discovering Heather's murderer than before. This entire Dane spectacle was a red herring."

"I don't know," I said. "I think there might be a connection." I turned to Trimble. "Shall we proceed?"

Trimble whispered to her second-in-command named John. He smiled and left the room.

A few minutes later, I heard the hallway door open and close. Familiar padding and wheezing sounded down the hall. Shaneika quietly shut the door to our room while I watched through the mirror.

Baby poked his head into the interrogation room looking for me when the woman in the white pantsuit spied him.

"Baby!" she cried, holding out her arms. "What are you doing here?"

Baby lifted his head in search of the person calling his name. Wagging his tail, Baby entered the interrogation room and went up to the woman, putting his head in her lap. She joyfully petted him while nattering "baby talk."

I said to Trimble, who was watching with me, "That

woman is Magda Dane McCloud."

"Crap!" Trimble mumbled.

Shaneika advised, "Bring the safe and ask her to open it. You will have evidence you can present. A dog being petted by a woman who likes dogs is not evidence. Just shows she likes dogs."

I made a face at Shaneika. "I think Baby letting this woman pet him is the best evidence."

"Well, here I go," Trimble said. She left us and entered the interrogation room, taking a seat opposite of the twin and turned on the tape recorder.

"My name is Sergeant Kate Trimble of the Kentucky State Police. I am conducting this interview at 1700 hundred hours. Please state your full name and address please."

"My name is Magda Dane McCloud. I live on Royster Island in Chesapeake Bay."

"Can you prove your identity as we have another woman stating that she is Magda Dane McCloud?"

"Maja will drop the charade as soon as she hears that I am here. My lawyer will be arriving soon to straighten this mess out as well."

"Can you prove that you are Magda Dane McCloud?"

"My personal assistant has informed me that you have taken a safe out of the Dane RV. She also told you that it requires an index finger imprint from Magda McCloud and only Magda McCloud." The woman held up both of her hands and wiggled her fingers. "As you can see, I have all ten of my digits intact."

"Very well," Trimble said. "I'll have the safe brought in but before we do, I'd like to ask a few questions."

"Shoot."

"Did you have anything to do with Heather Warfield's death?"

"I did not."

"Did your sister?"

"Of course not. My sister only knew her to say hello."

"Did your disappearance have anything to do with Heather Warfield's death?"

"No."

"You're admitting that you had disappeared for over twenty-four hours?"

"I was not kidnapped if that's what you mean."

"Where were you?"

"I was at a secret location in Baltimore signing papers for the sale of Dane Enterprises."

"Your sister, Margot, is under arrest for faking her ID and identity on an airline. That's a big no-no since 9/11."

Magda said, "The Defense Department will smooth this over. They don't want any of this in the papers."

"What does the Defense Department have to do with the sale of Dane Enterprises? I thought you had contracts with the Navy."

"Dane Enterprises has contracts with the Defense Department. For national security reasons I can't go further than to say that I have been receiving death threats due to the impending sale. I needed a decoy so Margot offered to act as me, while I chartered a private plane to Baltimore. The ruse worked. Unfortunately, my sister got caught up in the drama, but I will straighten it out."

"And Maja?"

"She also impersonated me while I was gone. I had to make people think I was still in Kentucky."

"She attacked your husband, Gavin. I think he is going to press charges."

"Gavin makes a big noise, but nothing will come of his threats. He's a problem I can throw some money at and make him go away. It doesn't matter anyway, since I'm going to divorce him."

"Was he to receive his copy of the divorce papers on Monday?"

"Yes, but I planned to be far away by then. I'm gathering my sisters and flying to our family compound until everything is settled."

"Was Gavin the one who was threatening you?"

"I did give the thought credence, but I haven't the proof. I think some disgruntled employees might have gotten a whiff of the sale and decided to make some waves. I have a detective working on the problem."

"What kind of threats were you receiving?"

"The usual. Emails to my office computer. Letters to my home address. Then I received a threatening text on a burner phone I keep. I felt I was being followed, even to Kentucky."

"Why not hire security?"

"How could I trust them? I would have to assume they weren't plants and I wasn't taking that chance. The only people I could trust were my sisters."

"How long have you been receiving threats?"

"Several months now."

"And you suspect Gavin?"

"Yes, I suspect him because of the texts sent to the burner phone. No one knew where I was this weekend. Not even my personal assistant."

"Did your sister want this deal to go through?"

"Maja knew I was burning out, exhausted. It's a good deal for all of us. The company will go public. Maja and I will have a place on the Board of Directors and all three sisters will retain stock in the company. We will have both power and money, but I won't have to work myself to death."

"Why did you zero in on Gavin?"

"I believe Gavin saw correspondence concerning the company's sale. Gavin has a prenup, and he will only get a fraction of what he would receive if he was a widower. I am seeking a divorce, and I think he suspects it's coming. We've been unhappy for a while, but I didn't leave him because it would have been bad for the business. The military likes stability."

"What story did you give Gavin to get him to go along with this cockamamie lie?"

"I told him that there had been an explosion at the factory and I had to get back. I explained to him that this needed to be kept quiet for the sake of the company. We have a new contract with the Navy and they might pull out if they thought Dane Enterprises were not up to it."

"So he threatened to tell."

"Yes, he blackmailed me so to speak, so I bribed him with money. Paid him two hundred thousand dollars to keep quiet. Money is the key to Gavin's heart."

"You know I have to verify all of this?"

Magda shrugged. "May I have a bottle of water?"

"Sure." Trimble called out for water. "Let's get back to this sale. If it was so important that you had to travel in secret about this deal, why did you tell Josiah Reynolds, Shaneika Todd, and Heather Warfield about it?"

"I had to have other pairs of eyes on the Dane family in case my plan went sideways. I had always planned to slip off and wanted someone other than the family to know what was happening."

"Why pick those three?"

"I had met Mrs. Reynolds previously and knew she

was a great friend of Lady Elsmere. Lady Elsmere has much influence and would back Josiah Reynolds if needed. There was another reason as well. Mrs. Reynolds is considered a great observer and is in the papers often for solving murders. If she said I was missing, the authorities would have to take notice. There was always a chance I was wrong about who was threatening me. I believed she would realize Maja was impersonating me and inform the police." Magda paused for a moment. "I hate to say this, but after Heather turned up dead, I believed she was mistakenly murdered for me. I felt it prudent to put my plan in place which I did."

"Heather Warfield told Josiah Reynolds she saw Gavin and Maja in the woods at dawn on Saturday morning conspiring to kill you."

"That's utter nonsense. Maja, Margot, Gavin, and I stayed at the B&B Friday night. That is when I told the family about the sale."

"But you believed Gavin might be behind sending you death threats?"

"Well, yes, but everyone was present at breakfast."

"What time was that?"

"Seven thirty."

"Enough time to get back to the B&B from Boonesborough." Trimble paused and looked at her notes. "From your answer, I'm getting the impression you and Gavin don't sleep together."

Magda brushed the question aside. "I'm sure the

B&B has some sort of surveillance camera, and the owners were up at six preparing breakfast. I'm sure they would know who came and went. Ask them."

"Did you see either Maja or Gavin between the hours of six and seven on Saturday morning?"

I could tell Magda was deciding whether to lie or not. Shaneika leaned toward the two-way mirror. Her face was contorted with anxiety. She was not alone in the anxiety department. My hands shook a little.

Magda sighed. "I did not."

A trooper brought in the safe and laid it on the table. Baby, who had been sitting quietly beside Magda, followed the man out and resumed his search for me. Shaneika opened the door to our little room. As soon as Baby got a whiff of me, he bounded joyfully into the room and bypassed Shaneika without giving her a glance. Shaneika snorted in derision. She had never been a big fan of my dog, and Baby knew it. I gave him a peanut butter treat from my pants pocket to compensate for Shaneika's lack of faith in him. Satisfied, Baby lay in a corner and fell asleep.

I turned just in time to see Magda punch in the security code and put her index finger on the scanner. The safe door slowly swung open.

"I have a warrant to examine the contents of this box."

Magda waved Trimble on. "Suit yourself. Nothing much in there."

Trimble pulled out three stacks of bills amounting to fifteen thousand dollars, a small .22 caliber pistol, and low and behold, a stun gun. "What have we here?"

Magda's eyes widened. "Those are mine. I forgot they were in there."

Trimble pulled on gloves taken from her shirt pocket and gingerly put the pistol and stunt gun into evidence bags, handing them to Trooper John Cymbala. "Get these to the lab and tell Amy I want these guns fingerprinted ASAP. Like in the next hour."

"Yes, ma'am."

Having regained her composure, Magda looked coolly at Trimble. "I would like to call my lawyer now. This interview is over."

"As you wish." Trimble grabbed the safe and walked out of the room, kicking the door shut with her foot.

Shaneika grabbed my arm in excitement, but I remained cautious.

The stun gun?

Not likely.

17

I took the liberty of Trimble's absence to creep into the interview room with Baby following me.

"I thought you had to be around," Magda said. "You and that dog are joined at the hip. I suppose you were watching behind the two-way mirror."

"You've got everyone riled up, Magda."

"It's just a simple misunderstanding."

"I don't think so."

Magda took out a compact from her purse and powdered her nose and then put on a fresh coat of dark red lipstick. The red lipstick contrasted beautifully with her ebony hair and alabaster skin. Dressed in her white raiment, Magda looked like a character out of a fairy tale. Snow White came to mind. Or maybe the Evil Queen.

"You are one cool customer."

"Josiah, I have no idea what you are talking about."

"I'm talking about the fact that Dane Enterprises underwrote this entire weekend for Dr. Reese. I saw the store clerk's check. It was issued from the Dane Corporation."

Magda slammed shut her compact and threw it back in her purse. "Dane Enterprises underwrites many charitable grants. We receive over two thousand applications per year and we select about four hundred for funding. Usually of short duration like this weekend dig. Dane Enterprises likes to be of service."

"You just happened to pick this one excavation out of all the applications you received this year."

"You're right about that. It was the perfect excuse to get away and have my family join me for the big news. I find it best to take people out of familiar surroundings when receiving life changing news. Besides, I wanted to see what farms were for sale. I really do want to move here. I'm tired of the East Coast."

"Is Gavin also something that you are tired of?"

"Of course, I'm tired of him. That's why I'm divorcing him."

I laughed. "I listened to your tale of woe of death threats, Gavin undermining you, Margot and Maja impersonating you, and it's all a bunch of bull. A red herring to confuse people. I know men. Gavin is more of a mouse than a lion. And why would he upset the apple cart? All he has to do is stay out of your way and look pretty when you need him."

"That's absurd."

"Why underwrite this dig? What was the true purpose of your visit?"

"If you must know, Allison and I go back years. We were in the same sorority at college. She asked me personally to fund this weekend, and I agreed. I saw no harm in it. It sounded fun."

"Ellison looks like Gavin's younger brother, and he's just your type—tall, dark, and very handsome. To add a cherry on top of the sundae, Ellison is smart. Some say brilliant in his field of expertise. I'm not saying Gavin is the dullest knife in the drawer, but he is dull to the point that he couldn't cut soft butter. Perhaps you were thinking of trading up. Since you and Dr. Reese go way back, she must have told you about Ellison's affairs, and that their marriage was ending."

"I don't have to listen to your wild suppositions."

"What was the plan, Magda? To play damsel in distress so Ellison would run to the rescue? Of course, Ellison would fall for you. You are beautiful with money to burn. Ellison would have been a fool not to accept your overtures. There was one thing standing in your way to seduce him. The plan went awry when you discovered there were other women at the dig with prior claims on Ellison. Sticky. Very sticky. And then there was the murder of Heather. You dropped your plans for Ellison like a hot potato. So much for love."

Magda waved her hand like a fluttering bird. "C'est la vie."

"It doesn't bother you that I am accusing you of being so shallow that you would betray an old friend by chasing after her skirt-chasing husband?"

"Everyone has to have a hobby."

"Wow, that's cold, even for a Dane."

"You can hurl insults at me all day long, Josiah. Doesn't bother me in the least. I long for the day when I can be shed free of Gavin. Boredom doesn't even describe what I feel when I'm with that man. Let me explain something about the Dane family—we take what we want. I wanted to use Ellison. Allison had no use for him anymore."

"I think Dr. Reese still loves him."

"She may, but their relationship is over. It's time for Allison to move on. One thing is for sure, Ellison doesn't love Allison. He used her as he does with all women. I thought it would be nice for a woman to use him for a change."

"It's not that I mind Ellison getting his comeuppance, but to do that to an old chum strikes me as chilling."

"You've never cheated? Never betrayed a friend over sex?"

I had to stop moralizing. I had betrayed a friend over sex, and the thing was I never regretted it. Who was I to judge? Still, I kept hammering. It was one thing to play naughty under the sheets, but another thing to snuff one's life out. "You do as you please, I see."

"That's right, but it sure doesn't include murder. I take pride in Dane Enterprises, and I've worked hard to make it a success. I would do nothing to compromise the family name or the company. Even we Danes have limits."

I scoffed.

"Oh, stop being a self-righteous prig. I know about you. You cross boundaries all the time, but you are right that I deliberately funded Allison Reese's pet project in order to see Ellison again. I was hoping to coax him into a compromising situation with me forcing Gavin to want a divorce, but Ellison never took the bait. Apparently, he was infatuated with someone else."

"Who?"

"Don't know."

"Were you even threatened?"

"Everything else I told you was true. I used this excavation to kill many birds with one stone—to force Gavin to want a divorce, to tell my sisters about the sale of the company, and to create a diversion."

"It sounds very complicated and foolish."

"I like to play games."

"And in doing so, you got Margot arrested, Maja arrested, and Gavin injured."

"I didn't anticipate the complications that would arise when your friend was murdered, but the plan had already been put into motion."

"How inconvenient for Heather to have died."

"My family had nothing to do with her death—this I swear."

"I hope you enjoy all that money you are going to receive for Dane Enterprises. It sure came at a high price for some people."

"Again, Josiah, you are too emotional. We had nothing to do with Heather's demise. You're just looking to blame someone."

Magda was right.

I did want to blame someone.

Somebody had to pay for Heather's death!

18

I convinced Sergeant Trimble to order a stakeout at the dig, revealing who I thought had killed Heather. In the end, it was only Shaneika, Sergeant Trimble, Trooper John Cymbala, who volunteered. I joined them hunkered down in the woods overlooking the dig.

Trimble flicked a penlight on her watch. "It's three in the morning. This is a waste of time."

"Turn that light off," I complained. "You're giving away our position."

"Shush both of you," Shaneika whispered. "These Palisades amplify sound."

"I'll give you both another half hour. No more," Trimble said.

Shaneika glared at Trimble. "Josiah is not usually wrong about these things. If she says the killer will show up, then the killer will show up."

"You make her sound like a human bloodhound."

"Hey guys, I'm right here. Now both of you keep your pie holes shut," I said in a low voice.

Trimble gritted her teeth. She hated working with civilians. Again, she was breaking protocol, but if she could bring in the killer, she could save this case and maybe her career.

Trimble settled in, as did Shaneika, who pulled her coat up around her neck. Trimble put on a pair of warm gloves she retrieved from her coat pocket. The night had turned cold as it was still spring. I had brought my sleeping bag, which I unzipped completely and spread over the backs of Trooper John Cymbala and myself. Being young, John had not thought to wear more appropriate clothing. I didn't mind sharing my converted sleeping bag with the young man. He smelled of fresh pine, which must have come from his aftershave lotion. It was nice. Of course, I would have been warmer if I had the sleeping bag to myself, but then snuggling up to a young, handsome male was not repugnant either. I may be old, but I'm not dead.

The four of us remained quiet until John pointed. "There's movement."

"Probably a bobcat or a bear," Trimble huffed.

"Everyone, be quiet." I leaned forward, straining my eyes. Even though I had grown accustomed to the dark, it was still hard to see.

John patted me on the shoulder and pointed again.

Shaneika tensed up as did Trimble. Out of the corner of my eye, I saw Trimble unsnap her gun holster.

A branch in the woods snapped. Then quiet—an

unearthly quiet as if the animals of the forest were holding their breath as well. Just the river could be heard rushing in the background.

We all strained to listen.

The rustle of dry leaves sounded as though someone was walking.

John threw off his portion of the sleeping bag and quietly stood up behind the tree we were under peering into the bare field where the dig had taken place. He also released his gun holster.

I wanted to tell them both that they wouldn't need their guns as this killer was a coward and would give up easily when confronted, but I remained silent. We had to catch this killer in the act.

A dark form emerged from the woods and paused, surveying the field and then the campgrounds. Everyone was asleep in their campers, and all dogs were safely tucked inside with their masters. The figure moved silently toward the excavation where the dirt had been plowed back and stooped, presumably to dig.

"Wait. Wait," I whispered cautiously as I sensed John was ready to make a move. "They have to have it on their person."

The person dug and dug without benefit of a flashlight for over ten minutes until an item was scooped up, dirt shaken off, and shoved in a pocket.

John was getting ready to make his move.

"Wait, John. Wait. Let her get away from the site," I

said softly, putting a restraining hand on his arm.

"She'll get away," Trimble said.

"She can't outrun John," I said. "Can she, John?"

"No ma'am. I was the fastest boy in high school. I've got medals to prove it."

"When I give you the signal, you are to move on the outside of the woods until you intercept her."

"She'll see me."

"Yes, she will and then she will turn. The rest of us will be coming up the rear and block her. No muss. No fuss."

We moved up to the trees outlining the field.

The figure stopped, searching the tree line.

The four of us froze. John looked at me waiting for the signal. I wondered if he could hear my heart beat.

Seeing nothing untoward, the figure began moving again across the field to the west side of the forest.

"Now!" I whispered.

John took off like a shot, but silent like a panther.

Trimble and Shaneika ran into the field with me trailing behind.

She spotted John, halted, and then turned only to run into Trimble and Shaneika. Changing directions again, she ran toward the campgrounds until Shaneika caught up with her. The two struggled until Trimble pulled her gun and yelled, "FREEZE! You are under arrest for the murder of Heather Warfield."

Shaneika got in one last punch until John caught up

and took control of the culprit.

Panting, I arrived just in time to hear Shaneika say, "Gotcha, bitch."

I looked into the face of the woman who had killed poor Heather. "Hello, Becky."

"What's this all about? Why are you arresting me? I haven't done anything," Becky protested.

"Why are you out here at four in the morning?" Trimble asked.

"I couldn't sleep. I wanted to make sure the site was covered correctly."

"Without a flashlight?"

"I have very good vision. I don't need a flashlight."

"Yeah, if you're a bat or vampire," Shaneika sneered.

Becky felt her cheek. "You hit me."

"You fell."

"No, you hit me, Shaneika. I'm going to press charges. Sergeant, arrest this woman for assaulting me."

Trimble replied, "No, you fell, Becky. Don't you remember?"

"Surely you saw Shaneika hit me?" Becky asked of John.

"Sorry, ma'am. I didn't see anything running after you. It was a blur."

Becky said, "I see how it is."

I was cold and tired. "Sergeant Trimble, I think you will find two pairs of earrings in one of her pockets that match the ones that I am wearing."

"You have no right to search me," Becky proclaimed as John cuffed her. "I have rights."

"Yes, you do," Trimble said. "You have the right to remain silent and the right to have an attorney present during interrogation. If you do not have an attorney, one will be assigned to you by the court. There—you've been Mirandized."

"The earrings?" I said.

"Miss Becky, do you have a weapon on your person or something that might injure me like a needle?"

"Go screw yourself."

"I guess that means I have to find out for myself." After putting on gloves, Trimble searched Becky and found two pairs of earrings in her left boot. She dangled them in her flashlight.

"They're agate," Shaneika said, peering at them.

"Do they have a red vein in them?" I asked.

"Yes, they do," Trimble answered, whipping out an evidence bag and placing the earrings in them. "We'll dust them for fingerprints."

Becky said, "Well, of course, my fingerprints are on them. I found those on the ground. Someone must have dropped them."

I said, "Yes, they were dropped by someone. Heather dropped them during the scuffle between Shaneika's RV and Heather's car. You're a very sloppy murderer, Becky. You left evidence everywhere.

Heather dropped her car keys as well. She must have been holding them in her hand and dropped them when she was tased, but you didn't see those when you came back to clean up the scene."

"I tell you I found those earrings on the ground."

"You weren't expecting Sergeant Trimble to search all the vehicles and campers in the campgrounds. She even searched the trash where she found the boxes that once held the earrings. You placed them in the trash barrel by the Dane's RV as to implicate them."

"You're reaching."

"Am I?"

"Look up there," I said pointing. "Sergeant Trimble put an infrared camera there and another one over there. We should have a good image of you digging up the earrings."

"I was just checking the site. You're making a big mistake here. I'll sue."

Ignoring Becky's protests, I continued, "You liked the earrings, so you kept them—a private reminder of how you put one over the rest of us. That is until, you saw my earrings and realized I had spoken with the gift shop clerk. You knew that I discovered Heather had purchased the earrings."

"You told me there was a tape of Heather buying the earrings. It's one of the reasons when I picked up the earrings, I knew they were important. I was going to turn them over to Sergeant Trimble," Becky said.

"Heather was going to give us those earrings Sunday night as a token of her affection," Shaneika said, her hands rolling into a fist.

"You know nothing of the kind," Becky said. "You are assuming. You know what they say about people who assume—making an ass out of you and me. Won't hold up in court."

I said, "Let me finish, Becky. You saw Trimble searching everyone. You had to get rid of them. No better place to stash them than in an excavated site when you could just wander over and drop them in the soil for the bulldozer to cover. You marked the spot, so you could come back when the heat was off and Trimble had stopped searching the area, but you couldn't risk them being found at a future date."

"For the last time, I found them on the ground."

Shaneika asked, "Why did you murder Heather? She hadn't done anything to you."

"I didn't."

"You did and you had help. There is no way you could have moved Heather's body to the river yourself. Heather was a big girl."

"Again I say—prove it."

"You set my RV on fire."

"Again I say—prove it."

Shaneika said, "Sergeant Trimble made a deal with Ellison last night. He's singing like a nightingale."

Becky's eyes widened. Suddenly, she looked frightened. "You're trying to trick me. Ellison was released."

Trimble said, "He has been charged as an accessory to murder. He's made a deal and left you swinging in the wind."

"Why do you keep bringing up Ellison? He's nothing to me."

I said, "He's everything to you, Becky. Ellison is a serial adulterer. As soon as he's finished with one woman, he goes on to the next. Heather was one of his lovers. She really loved him."

"You call that love? She was obsessed with him."

"Now, how would you know that?" Shaneika asked. "Heather was discreet and only three people knew of Heather's feelings for Ellison—Dr. Reese, Ellison, and me."

Becky stammered, "You—you could tell how she felt. She was always making cow eyes at him."

I countered, "I worked this weekend with Heather, and I never picked up on her feelings for Ellison. It was only later that I learned about their affair, but that's not why you killed her."

"You're talking rubbish."

"Oh, I think Heather coming this weekend bothered you, since you knew about her past with Ellison, but that's not why you killed her. You killed Heather because she overheard you and Ellison planning to murder Dr. Reese."

Becky's face reddened as she struggled with John.

"Miss Rebecca, if you kick me again, I'll have to shackle your feet," John said, tightening his hold on her.

"Why would I want to hurt Dr. Reese? I work for her, you idiot."

"Heather went for an early morning walk just at dawn. She stumbled across you and Ellison in the woods, but with her poor eyesight and it not being quite light yet, she mistook you for one of the Dane twins and Ellison for Gavin. You are petite like the Dane twins and Ellison is tall and dark like Gavin."

"Well, there again, you fall short. She would have recognized my voice."

"Well, there again, Becky, why are you assuming she heard a woman's voice and not the man's unless you were there? I think Heather was in shock and didn't realize whom she really had seen. You didn't know Heather had mistaken you two for Gavin and Maja. You concluded you had to get rid of her. So you lured her out of the RV. Then you killed Heather and got Ellison to help you throw that poor besotted woman into the river."

"Conjecture. No proof."

"You made several mistakes like telling me that you had found Heather's body and reported it to the camp manager."

"I did."

"I talked with the camp manager myself, Becky, and

he says you never spoke to him about Heather."

"He's an older man. He's just forgotten."

Trimble spoke up, "I talked with the kayakers. They denied seeing you when they discovered Heather, and the camp manager confirmed that they informed him about Heather—not you."

"You had to establish a plausible reason why you were near the river if someone saw you," Shaneika said.

"I'm not saying another word without my lawyer," Becky hissed.

"Okay," Trimble said, nodding to John.

Shaneika said hurriedly, "One thing that puzzles me is why you set my RV on fire."

"Did I? Prove it."

John pulled Becky away and marched her over to an unmarked police SUV parked beside the Dane's RV.

"What do you think?" Shaneika asked of Trimble.

"I think we better haul Dr. Reese in and have a private chat with her. She may hold the key to this mess."

"I guess this means the Danes are innocent," Shaneika said.

"I don't think they had anything to do with Heather. They were too busy with their own drama," Trimble said. "Margot Dane will still be charged, but I'm sure the Dane's highfalutin lawyers will get her off on some technicality." She yawned. "At the moment, I'm going home to get some sleep. We'll bring in Dr. Reese this afternoon for a little chat."

"I would like to be there," Shaneika said.

"No can do. I'm sticking to protocol from here on out."

"Going to bed sounds like a good idea," I said. "I need some shut eye. Come on, Shaneika. Let's go."

Shaneika and I left Trimble and headed for our RV. I really needed to sleep and so did Shaneika.

We were both running on empty. We needed to be bright-eyed and bushy-tailed for the afternoon.

Sergeant Trimble didn't know it, but Shaneika and I were going to be at that interview.

We just needed to come up with a plan.

19

Trimble picked up her file as John knocked on her office door.

"Dr. Reese is here," he said. "I've put them in the interview room."

"Them?"

"She brought her lawyer with her."

"Great. Just great." Trimble sighed, picking up her coffee cup in her other hand. "Well, let's put this case to bed."

Trimble went into the interview room and stopped in mid stride.

Sitting in a scarred metal chair was Dr. Reese and beside her sat Shaneika.

"What are you doing here?" Trimble asked briskly.

"You asked me to come," Dr. Reese said.

"No, I mean her," Trimble said, pointing at Shaneika.

"I'm Dr. Reese's lawyer."

"You can't be."

Shaneika replied, smiling, "Actually, I can. There is nothing in the statutes prohibiting me."

"May we proceed, please?" Dr. Reese asked. "I have another appointment I need to attend."

"What appointment?"

"It's personal. I'd rather not say."

"Dr. Reese, you are involved in a murder investigation. There is no such thing as privacy in regards to murder."

Dr. Reese whispered to Shaneika to which she responded, "I think you should cooperate with Sergeant Trimble. She has news for you that might not be pleasant, but you need to hear."

Dr. Reese turned to Trimble. "Is this an official interrogation?"

"It's just a talk. Conversation among three gals."

"Very well, then. I have an appointment with a divorce lawyer. I am signing my divorce papers."

"What happens to Ellison when you divorce him, Dr. Reese?"

"Ellison's a grown man. He'll get by."

"I mean what is he losing by not being married to you?"

"I don't understand. What are you trying to say?"

"If you were to die, what would Ellison gain? How would he profit?"

Disturbed, Dr. Reese thought for a moment before answering. "My family is one of the original families from Fort Boonesboro. I am the sole surviving descendant. I'm not rich like the Danes, but I'm well off. Ellison would inherit family money, a drafty antebellum mansion, and a hundred acres of prime Bluegrass hosting a couple of rundown barns. It looks glamorous from the outside, but takes a lot of money for upkeep."

"Anything else?"

"I would have taken Ellison's name off the book we were writing about early Kentucky history. It would have been a blow to his career. He needed the attribution to springboard him to the next level. Ellison was hoping to get a full time professorship at the university. He is very ambitious. This book would have put him ahead of the competition as it was going to be controversial and would have garnered him much attention in his field." Dr. Reese glanced at Shaneika for confirmation.

"And Ellison was aware that you were divorcing him?"

"Of course. We have been separated for over a year, and he knew I was to sign the official papers today. He had already signed his and submitted them to my lawyer for filing."

Shaneika said, "Once Dr. Reese signs her divorce papers, and her lawyer files them, the divorce is a fait accompli."

Staring at Shaneika, Trimble said, "I thought you were Dr. Reese's lawyer."

"I don't handle divorce cases," Shaneika retorted, giving Trimble a slick smile.

"Why are you divorcing Ellison? Was it to do with Heather Warfield?"

"Oh, poor Heather. She was just one of many Ellison trifled with. Women were his hobby. He went through them like tissue paper. It didn't matter what they looked like either. I would say he was very democratic about that. As long as they had a pulse and wore lipstick, he was on them like a tick on a hound. I knew about the others, but Ellison was discreet, so I wasn't humiliated in public. It wasn't that way with Heather. When I caught them in my bed, it was too much. I could no longer pretend Ellison wasn't cheating on me. He didn't love me. I had to face that fact."

"What happened with Ellison after you caught him?"

"He threw Heather off and begged me for another chance, but I knew he wouldn't change. Ellison could not stay away from the ladies."

Trimble said, "He was having an affair with Becky."

"Doesn't surprise me."

"You knew?"

"I suspected, but after Ellison left the house, I paid little attention to him. I was over him. No need to talk to him except about work. My divorce lawyer handled the details about other matters."

"I think things got a little strange with Becky."

"What do you mean?"

"According to Ellison, Heather was killed because she overhead him and Becky planning to murder you."

"WHAT!" Dr. Reese stood, knocking her chair back.

While Trimble called out for a glass of water, Shaneika put the chair to right and motioned for Dr. Reese to sit down.

Trooper John Cymbala, who had been observing behind the two-way mirror, fetched a bottle of water for Dr. Reese and Shaneika before returning to his spot.

After taking several sips, Dr. Reese regained her composure and asked, "Why? Why would Ellison contemplate such a thing? He is a brilliant botanist. He can find a position anywhere."

"Apparently, Ellison wanted the drafty antebellum mansion with the hundred acres hosting two rundown barns. And the family money was icing on the cake. Most of all, he wanted that book published with his name on it."

"I don't believe it."

"How much was the family money?"

"Seven hundred thousand."

"People have killed for less."

"Ellison is an adulterer. He's not a murderer. He's a very passive male when it comes to violence. I just don't see it."

"Maybe not, but with Becky pushing the agenda, he became one. Sometimes the dynamics of a relationship breathe life into an evil agenda that otherwise would never had been pursued. Would Bonnie have robbed banks without her Clyde?"

Shaneika asked, "Did Ellison confess to killing Heather?"

Trimble said, "Becky killed Heather. Lured her out of the RV by telling Heather that Josiah had been in a car accident."

"How do you know that?" Shaneika asked.

"Ellison told us," Trimble replied. "Ellison was only involved by helping Becky dispose of the body, but that makes him an accessory after the fact."

Dr. Reese hung her head. "That's what Ellison says, but can you believe him?"

"Did you cut a plea deal with him?" Shaneika cut in.

"The DA is working on his statement now. If they find it to be credible, they'll make a deal. If he testifies against Becky, he'll get a much lighter sentence."

Dr. Reese asked, "What about the plan to murder me?"

"No charge will be brought on that. The only person that witnessed the conversation is dead, and both Ellison and Becky will not say a word about it."

Shaneika asked, "Then what was the motive for murdering Heather?"

"Becky blames Ellison. Said it was because Heather

caught them making love in the woods. They didn't want their affair exposed, so Ellison murdered Heather on his own. Becky is claiming her innocence. It's 'she said' versus 'he said.' Without more evidence, the DA can't charge either one of them for Heather's murder. It's too circumstantial."

Shaneika coughed and pushed back in her chair. "You know that's a lie."

Dr. Reese turned to Shaneika. "Heather didn't tell you what she heard?"

Trimble answered, "Miss Warfield told Josiah Reynolds what she overheard, but the DA thinks Mrs. Reynolds' testimony would be too weak. It is considered third hand and is without any other witnesses or evidence to corroborate it."

"Will Ellison and Becky get out on bail?" Dr. Reese asked, looking alarmed. She pulled a handkerchief from her purse and patted the sweat from her face.

"Most probably," Trimble assured. "I'm sorry."

Dr. Reese pleaded, "Are we done here? I don't know anything more. I need to get to my divorce lawyer's office. I can't sign those divorce papers soon enough."

Trimble stood and closed her file. "I'm sorry we can't press more charges against Ellison, but the law's the law. If I were you, I'd hide out or hire a bodyguard until those divorce papers are filed."

Dr. Reese and Shaneika stood.

Trimble offered, "Ms. Todd, I never expressed this, but I'm sorry for the death of your cousin."

"Thank you. I appreciate it."

"It's that damn fort's fault," Dr. Reese sputtered. "Do you know how many died to save that fort and those who died trying to destroy it! I hate it. I wish I had never gotten that grant to dig there."

Trimble and Shaneika looked astonished at Dr. Reese's outburst.

Dr. Reese continued, "The ground around that fort is soaked with the blood of innocents. I'm not surprised that it wanted one more sacrifice. That piece of land is ground zero for Kentucky being the 'dark and bloody ground.' Daniel Boone was warned about Kentucky's lust for blood by Dragging Canoe at the signing of the Treaty of Sycamore Shoals, but Boone was too dazzled by Kentucky to listen—too much good farming land, water, and game to resist. Two hundred plus years later we are still paying the price for our ancestors' folly. Kentucky should have been abandoned by the frontiersmen like the indigenous population had done years before. They only came to Kentucky to hunt."

Shaneika picked up Dr. Reese's purse. "You've had a shock. I'm going to drive you to your divorce lawyer and then take you to a safe place until this mess is over. We'll stop by your house and pick up a few things."

Dr. Reese nodded as Shaneika wrapped her arm

around the rattled archaeologist and led her to Shaneika's car.

Sergeant Trimble and Trooper John Cymbala followed and watched Shaneika drive away.

John said, "You solved the case. I guess you'll get your promotion to lieutenant now."

"I won't relish it. It's hard to accept one's success at the cost of another's misfortune."

John grinned. "I'll guess you'll get over it."

Trimble watched Shaneika turn the corner and drive out of sight. "I guess I will, but it's a hell of a thing. Yep, it's a hell of a thing." She turned and went inside with John trailing after her. As far as Trimble was concerned, the Warfield case was closed as soon as the paperwork was finished. It was in the DA's hands now.

Good luck with that.

20

Lady Elsmere, my next door neighbor, and I stood on the portico of the Big House, waiting for Shaneika and Dr. Reese to arrive. Since Lady Elsmere knew Dr. Reese better than Shaneika and I, we thought it best to hide her here. There was a guest suite next to Lady Elsmere's bedroom where the archaeologist would be safe and comfortable, able to still work on her book. If Dr. Reese needed to run errands, it was decided that Malcolm (an heir of Lady Elsmere's) would drive and accompany her wherever she went. This was to continue until Dr. Reese received word that the divorce had been finalized. After that, Ellison would have no reason to kill her, unless it was out of spite.

Dr. Reese got out of the car and stared at the Big House, a huge antebellum mansion my late husband, Brannon, had restored.

"Welcome," Lady Elsmere said, holding out her hands. "So good to see you again, Dr. Reese. I'm so sorry that we meet under such circumstances."

Dr. Reese climbed the limestone steps to greet Lady Elsmere. "Your Ladyship, it's so decent of you to take me in on such short notice and for practically a stranger. We've only met at university functions. I feel like I'm putting you out, but Shaneika insisted."

"It's no problem at all. It's not the first time I've had guests that had to 'lay low' so to speak."

"Of course, you know my sorority sister, Magda Dane McCloud. I understand she has attended several of your famous Derby parties, Lady Elsmere."

"No need for formalities. Call me June, please. We girls have to stick together." Lady Elsmere gave Dr. Reese a big hug.

"Call me Allison, please." Dr. Reese turned toward me. "Hello, Josiah."

"Tough day I understand."

"Awful, but I'll muddle through. It was just a shock to learn my spouse was planning to murder me."

Lady Elsmere said, "After a nap and a good meal, you will feel right as rain. You'll put this behind you and soar. Have I ever told you about the time I almost let a forger swindle me? He was a portrait painter, and I let him stay in my house. Imagine having a predator in one's own home and I was the one who insisted upon it. And he tried to steal my jewels, the swine, but Josiah caught him with stolen paintings from WWII or rather, her daughter, Asa, did. Almost got shot for it, too."

"The jewel thief was another man, June. It was during the citywide couture exhibit."

"Oh, yes, indeed, it was. Josiah and I have had so many adventures together, I can't keep straight all the villains we have put in jail. So you see, my dear, this is just a bump in the road. Just a bump. You'll recover and get on with your life." Lady Elsmere shivered. "Let's go inside. I'm getting a chill. Need some hot tea with a little shot of something extra, eh." She nudged Dr. Reese with her elbow.

Shaneika retrieved Dr. Reese's suitcase and lugged it up the steps.

"How did it go?" I asked.

"She took it better than expected. I wish she was angrier about Ellison. Dr. Reese seems more frightened than anything."

"It was a good idea to bring Dr. Reese here. I don't think Ellison would think to look for her here."

"Has she signed the divorce papers?"

"I took her straight from Trimble to her divorce lawyer. We just need to wait until the divorce is finalized."

"When will that be?"

"When it crawls through the bureaucratic system. Who knows? Today. Three weeks from now."

"This didn't turn out as I expected. I thought for sure the Dane sisters had something to do with it."

Shaneika laughed. "The great Josiah Reynolds couldn't figure out who-done-it."

"I figured it out in the end."

"Your name won't get into the papers this time. The judge has put a gag order on it."

"I bet Trimble had something to do with that. She can't afford to share the credit if she wants to make lieutenant."

"Do you think Ellison would have really gone through with killing Dr. Reese?"

"I think Becky would have egged Ellison on. Nasty little bugger she is."

"I have another name for her that starts with a 'B.'"

I laughed. "Hey, next time, you get a burr up your fanny about volunteering for an archaeological excavation, leave me out. Okay?"

A phone rang.

"That's you," I said.

Shaneika put down the suitcase and reached into her pocket. "Hello." She listened intently. "Yes, I understand. I'll make sure she knows."

"Who is it?" I asked, after seeing Shaneika's face fall.

She motioned for me to be quiet.

I waited patiently for Shaneika to end the call, and when she did, I pounced.

"You should see your face. Bad news?"

"That was Trimble. Ellison was found dead floating in the Kentucky River at Fort Boonesborough this afternoon. Had been shot. Trimble thinks it was suicide, but they are doing a complete autopsy workup."

"Has Becky been released on bail?"

"Seems so."

"Well, there's your answer of how Ellison was shot."

"Maybe. Maybe not."

"Jumping Jehoshaphat! That damned fort."

Shaneika said, "Tell me about it."

"Do you think Ellison committed suicide?"

"Really? No. We are on the same page thinking Becky killed him out of spite. They're looking for her now. Good thing we've hidden Dr. Reese. This news is going to be a shock for sure."

"Yeah, but what about us?" I asked. "We're sitting ducks for that loon."

Shaneika and I turned to look at Tates Creek Road. From our high vantage point on the portico, we could see cars through the trees speeding on the road.

I suddenly felt vulnerable and picked up Dr. Reese's suitcase. "Let's go inside."

"Agree," Shaneika said.

As soon as we were over the threshold, I slammed the double door shut and locked it. I looked at my watch. "It's tea time. June and Dr. Reese will be in the library."

I followed Shaneika into the walnut paneled library where the two ladies were chatting amiably.

Shaneika said, "Dr. Reese, I've got something to tell you. I'm afraid it's bad."

Dr. Reese looked up expectantly. Fear grew in her face as Shaneika strode over to her.

I closed the door to the library and prepared myself for the outpouring of grief from Dr. Reese that was to come, all the while thinking Chief Dragging Canoe was right—Kentucky is truly a "dark and bloody ground."

Keep on reading!

A Little Bit of History

After the end of the French and Indian Wars (1754-1763), King George III issued the Royal Proclamation of 1763 stating that Euro-Americans could not cross westward over the Appalachian Mountains into what was considered Native American territory. Negotiating with Native Americans for land rights or settling in their territory was forbidden and illegal. This was due partly to the unrest the British were experiencing with coastal Americans over taxation and the expense of providing protection for settlers.

Long hunter Daniel Boone was among a handful of men who defied the Proclamation and visited "Kentah-ten" which means "land of tomorrow" on several occasions. Due to his prowess in the woods and his familiarity with Kentucky, Boone was hired by Richard Henderson and eight other men, who had formed the Transylvania Company, to cut a road using the Athiamiowee or Warrior's Path through the Appalachian Mountains to the south side of the Kentucky River. This road was little more than a cleared pathway. The Transylvania Company's purpose was to establish a new colony.

Relying on mounting unrest in the East and intent upon beating other land speculators to the punch, Henderson met with Cherokee Indians at Sycamore Shoals and purchased 16 million acres south of the Kentucky River to the northern boundary of the Cumberland River for the cost of two thousand pounds in trading goods.

It was at Sycamore Shoals that Dragging Canoe warned Daniel Boone that a dark and bloody cloud hung over "Ken-tah-ten." Although Dragging Canoe's father, Attakullakulla, signed the treaty, Dragging Canoe broke away and became known as a war chief attacking Euro-settlers.

After the treaty was signed, Boone established Fort Boonesborough as the headquarters for the Transylvania Company. Richard Henderson's land purchase was considered illegal, and eventually the Transylvania Company lost all claims to the land. However, Euro-Americans, in their lust for land, flooded Kentucky walking the Wilderness Road or floating down the Ohio River on flatboats.

Other Native American tribes refused to give up their claims to Kentucky, thus creating a crisis when European frontiersmen began arriving with their families. This resulted in years of warfare and bloodshed.

Native American resistance to European settlers in

Kentucky and the Ohio Valley regions basically ended with the death of the great Shawnee chief, Tecumseh, at the Battle of the Thames in 1813.

I don't need to tell you the rest of the story. You know the ending.

Books By Abigail Keam

Death By A HoneyBee I
Death By Drowning II
Death By Bridle III
Death By Bourbon IV
Death By Lotto V
Death By Chocolate VI
Death By Haunting VII
Death By Derby VIII
Death By Design IX
Death By Malice X
Death By Drama XI
Death By Stalking XII
Death By Deceit XIII
Death By Magic XIV
Death By Shock XV

The Mona Moon Mystery Series
Murder Under A Blue Moon I
Murder Under A Blood Moon II
Murder Under A Bad Moon III
Murder Under A Silver Moon IV
Murder Under A Wolf Moon V
Murder Under A Black Moon VI

Last Chance For Love Romance Series
Last Chance Motel I
Gasping For Air II
The Siren's Call III
Hard Landing IV
The Mermaid's Carol V

About The Author

Hi, I'm Abigail Keam. I write the award-winning *Josiah Reynolds Mystery Series* and the *Mona Moon 1930s Mystery Series*. In addition, I write *The Princess Maura Tales* (Epic Fantasy) and the *Last Chance For Love Series* (Sweet Romance).

I am a professional beekeeper and have won awards for my honey from the Kentucky State Fair. I live in a metal house with my husband and various critters on a cliff overlooking the Kentucky River. I would love to hear from you, so please contact me.

Until we meet again, dear friend, happy reading!

You can purchase books directly from my website: www.abigailkeam.com